Planting Daisies

Planting Daisies

When Roses Just Won't Do . . .

Robin K. Johnson

Foreword by
Ron Clark

RESOURCE *Publications* • Eugene, Oregon

PLANTING DAISIES
When Roses Just Won't Do . . .

Resource Publications
An Imprint of Wipf and Stock Publishers
199 W. 8th Ave., Suite 3
Eugene, OR 97401

www.wipfandstock.com

ISBN 13: 978-1-62564-894-5

Manufactured in the U.S.A.

To Callie

Contents

Foreword

LIFE IS AS DIVERSE as the flowers in a field, especially those in which daisies are planted. Daisies overtake a field and provide a sense of beauty. Each flower is unique, but when one surveys the field, each seems just like every other flower. Looking over a meadow of these daisies provides spectacular views of God's blessing upon all creation. But when we look closer, we see the individual glory of each blossom.

Daisies are common flowers. Some would say that they are not as impressive as roses, orchids, or magnolias. Others simply believe that their value is in their distinct, yet similar appearance. They are all special, but only to someone who takes the time to look closely.

In my years in ministry I have learned to handle emotional mood swings between joy and sadness, grief and humor, as well as cynicism and hope. Like daisies, human lives are unique, though they may sometimes seem all alike. Each person's stories affect those who listen and care. My decades of ministry have given me the opportunity to listen to many people's stories, hopes, and dreams. Whether my wife and I are hearing confessions from behind the bars of a prison or listening to the deep trauma of survivors of abuse, the excuses of someone in the throes of addiction, the suffering of a cancer patient and their spouse, or the stories of children, we have learned that people are a field of daisies. Some see such people and their simple stories as commonplace, but those of us who look closely, listen intently, and offer acceptance know that they are all unique.

Planting Daisies is an encounter with those whom we have neglected to take the time to meet in our day-to-day lives. These are stories I have personally heard in other fields, from daisies that few have had the opportunity to appreciate. These are real people with real struggles, humor, and dreams. They are the common men, women, and children in our neighborhoods, schools, and churches who we have been forgotten or ignored. Their stories are each unique, yet altogether similar. They are tragic, yet hopeful.

Robin K. Johnson takes us on a journey into the homes, porches, cells, courtrooms, and offices where these daisies grow. Those who watch from a distance believe they are all the same. To such people, they are just another story on the news, in the paper, or in the church bulletin. Those who will take the time to read on will be moved by the compassion, anger, love, and fear that these daisies experience. With raw language, emotion, and faith, Johnson will lead you to examine each blossom closely to realize they are each unique in their struggle for survival as well as their hope for something better. *Planting Daisies* will draw us to compassion, empathy, and love for others while maintaining the dignity of each individual flower.

I look forward to reading this book again and again.

Dr. Ron Clark
Agape Church of Christ
Portland, OR

1
Fledglings

I THOUGHT THAT I WAS DREAMING. WE HAD A GOOD NIGHT TO-gether. Our girls were across the street at a sleepover. We ate dinner and took in a movie and walked around the block just to talk about our fifteen years together. The time had gone so fast that the little things in life that had made us angry then now seemed to be just small occurrences in all of the ups and downs we had been through. She shook me awake, making me think she wanted to go for it again.

"Did you hear that?" Callie whispered to me. "I think some-body is in the house."

I jumped out of bed and made my way to the den. I was still struggling to get the sleep out of my eyes. I slid my feet into my ten-nis shoes and headed for the door. My wife was on her knees trying to open the bottom drawer of her nightstand without making too much noise.

"Wait for me, I've got to get my little friend."

"Hush, I got this," I whispered in my manliest tone even though I was scared as hell. My heart was in my stomach, but I was furious that someone was in my house, taking my stuff and maybe planning to hurt my family.

"Boy, you better think about who you are talking to." My wife and her military weapons training. Always bringing that up.

"I guess you want to wear the big drawers too?"

I left the room and found myself tiptoeing through the house trying to scan the darkness. The little night-lights we have in the hallways didn't give off enough light to be any help. I was armed with the little oak bat that I made back in high school shop class. I had improved the strength of the bat by adding a twelve-inch bolt down the center after boring a hole into its two-foot core. I knew it would come in handy—I just thought that it would have been in my old high school's parking lot.

I got to the den, where someone screamed at me to get out of his way. I hit him two or three times, not stopping to wonder whether he might have partners in our house.

Pop! Pop!

I felt the warmth of blood running down my front. The pain crept into my mind as I tried to swing again.

"You bastards have broken into the wrong damn house!" My wife is very outspoken.

Pop! Pop! Pop! Her .380 was doing most of the talking for her.

I heard screams and breaking glass as I hit the coffee table and then the floor. I saw my wife firing her gun several more times before I realized that I had been hurt so badly that I was becoming too dizzy to see.

Pop! Pop! Pop! Pop!

"Oh yeah, I hit one of those bastards. I know I did." She dropped the clip and put a new one in the gun. "Baby, are you okay? Did I hit you by mistake?"

"No . . ." Though my lips still struggled to form the words, I couldn't get anything else out.

"Stay still, I'm gonna call 911." Things went black for a minute, but I could still hear her voice. It sounded muffled. "Yes, I do have a gun. I hit one of them. It was three of them in a brown car and another car pulled out right after them." Then all sound faded away . . .

———

I was baffled by the way everyone was moving around. It seemed so slow and methodical. The police seemed to be asking my wife the same questions. The answers she was giving didn't seem to satisfy the curiosity of why someone would break into our home. I felt hands on me and something on my face was stopping me from breathing easily. They kept grabbing my arms and telling me to lie still. All I could think was that I had to get to my feet and help my wife explain this mess.

"Ma'am, the permit for your gun is too tattered to read all of the pertinent information. You will need to have this replaced. When did you say you purchased the gun?"

"Like I've been *saying* for the past fifteen minutes," she drawled, rolling her eyes, "I've had that .380 since college."

"What college was that?"

"The college of *I ain't gonna be vulnerable again.*" She had hit her limit. I wanted to laugh, but nothing came out. The paramedics did laugh as they picked up my body and laid me on the gurney, where I could just make out the neighbors coming out in their pajamas to investigate the flashing lights and sirens.

"Ma'am, this is a serious matter. We need to get all the information from you that we can to solve this situation."

"You don't think I know that this is serious? I shot someone. Someone shot my husband." I saw her eyes follow the medics as they rolled me out the door and onto the driveway. "Cailyn, ride in that ambulance with your dad."

Callie turned back to the officer. "Or are you just daft?" Ignoring the officer's answer, she turned to our daughter, saying, "Pray, okay?"

Cailyn moved as quickly as she was told.

"I was already doing that," our daughter answered as she locked worried eyes with her mother over my gurney.

As they rolled me to the ambulance, I saw my neighbor's car screeching to a halt. The smell of burned tires wafted across the yard. I knew that "Two" was home, and she was mad. Two is my fifteen-year-old daughter, Rebekah. She doesn't put up with too much mess from anybody.

"We got them buttheads!" she shouted as she exited the driver's side of the car. "We got them buttheads!"

"Ma'am, stop right there." The short, fat officer approached her. "Who did you get?"

Two handed him a piece of paper and looked over to the ambulance. Cailyn gave her sister the okay sign and climbed in after they wheeled me in.

"We got the fools that broke into my parents' house." Two was very loud, much louder than usual when she's upset about something. "Here's the number off the truck they were in. Me, my sister, Mikkel, and the other girls in the car were across the street at a sleepover. We were up late talking and laughing out by the Moons' pool when Dee Dee saw that truck stop at the end of our driveway. We watched as they looked around and ran straight for the patio doors. I was hoping they wouldn't be able to get in, but things happened so fast!" She looked over to my wife and gave a little smile. "All we heard was my mom cursing and shooting. We saw the guys run out and get into the truck. One of them was holding his face and it sounded like he was crying. Then they got into the truck and took off fast."

"So how did you get them?" The policeman handed the paper off to a younger officer, who got on the radio as he walked away.

"We got in the station wagon and chased them." She shrugged her shoulders as if it were a normal thing to do. "How do you think you guys got the call to come out here? Amber dialed as we pulled off after them fools and Mikkel and Dee Dee loaded up the flare guns."

"Flare guns?" He looked as puzzled as I felt. He wrote on his little pad and looked at her as if she were the one in trouble. "You said flare guns?"

"Yeah, we needed some type of weapon. So we took them out of the Moons' boat as we ran to the car." She looked at her mother. "The women at Daisy told us to always be looking for a weapon to protect ourselves." She looked back at her friends and continued. "We were protecting our interests, right?

"Where are the flare guns?" Two ignored the question. He scribbled something else on his little pad.

"We followed them as close as we could—"

"They were booking it too," Dee Dee chimed in, interrupting Two. "I would say they hit ninety miles an hour when they turned on MLK. But our old station wagon kept up."

"She sure did!" Two continued, "I was already mad. So when they stopped, I rolled up, took the flare from Dee Dee and took the first shot into the windows."

"Yeah, we got off a couple of shots!" Dee Dee and Mikkel sang out in unison.

"A couple of shots?" The officer looked up at his partner and then back at the girls gathered in front of him. "Flares only load one shot at a time. How did you get off a couple of shots?"

"It was two of us loading." Mikkel looked at the girls and then motioned at the Moons coming over from across the street. "Yeah, I shot off three rounds, and Dee Dee . . . I think Dee Dee got maybe four."

"I got off six." The girl stuck out her chest like she was Annie Oakley. "I ain't playing."

The girls smiled at each other.

"So, where are the flare guns and the guys you followed?" he asked, looking pointedly at Two.

"After we pulled off and turned around, we saw them go into the third house from the corner of Lieght Street and Magnolia."

"Shoot, they just have to be hurt," Dee Dee said.

"Hurt and burnt," Mikkel added.

"Who are you?" He looked at my fourteen-year-old.

"I am Mikkel. This is my house." She looked at my wife and smiled.

"You know, you girls could possibly be in a little trouble." He motioned for other officers. "We'll have to take your statements at the station."

"You'll get them later," Callie said as she moved over to our car. "Two, you and Mikkel get in this car, now!"

"Ma'am?" The officer tried to address my wife. She was done talking.

"'Ma'am' nothing! I know you just watched my husband get rolled into that ambulance, and I don't intend to be far behind." She started the car and looked over at the Moons. "Please have someone watch our house?"

"We will." Mr. Moon waved her away. "Just go!" Two climbed into the backseat next to Mikkel.

I looked around the neighborhood. I saw more than half my neighbors standing in my front yard. I couldn't make sense of a word that anyone was saying. All I could hear was my daughter, Cailyn, quietly praying through her tears as the ambulance began to make its way toward the hospital.

"Ma'am, you can't just leave here like that. This is a crime scene. I have questions."

"Look, don't be as silly as I think you are." Callie was not happy. "You can meet me at the hospital anytime." She drove off.

———

"Man, look at the bumper of her car." The officer he had called over was cluing him in to things I had known about my wife for years.

"What does it mean? It's just a small yellow daisy."

"Man, you don't want to get into any mess with any of those women. They will rip you a new one."

"Are they on the job?"

"No, they are a rape counseling center like you have never known. There are a lot of rumors, but no one has anything on them. They are serious about the things they deal with and the women who have gone through there are all off, if you ask me. Just let it go and meet her at the hospital after we secure this scene."

"Okay," he answered, clearly now knowing what he was in for.

———

As the pain got worse, my consciousness began to fade. I felt my mind leave the blaring ambulance and found myself looking over my little family as they rushed toward the hospital's parking lot. I could see their love for me on the anxious expressions gripping their faces. No one spoke to each other. The car was filled with the tearful silence of unspoken prayers. It was like watching Hannah of the Bible speak to God. I could see their lips moving, but no words broke the silence. For a second, just a second, I thought that they were afraid to pray in front of each other. But that was a crazy thought. We had been praying with one another twice a week for years now.

———

The emergency room was bright and loud. People kept asking me questions that I couldn't answer. My lips weren't working. I just kept looking around the room trying to get my bearings. They were poking and prodding my body, sticking needles in my arms and touching my face. They seemed to be talking about a great deal of nothing. The only thing that was really irking me was that constant and continuous beeping. I wanted to tell somebody to shut that stifling noise off, but I didn't know these people like that. I had to maintain a good Christian image because I was in mixed company.

They x-rayed me several times. They gave me shot after shot. They asked me if my stomach hurt. They told me that I would feel a sharp stick and some pressure. They told me to be strong because my family had just arrived—as if I hadn't been busy being strong for them for the past fifteen years. That dang-gum beeping finally went off. I couldn't see them or the bright lights of the emergency room.

I opened my eyes and felt my wife's hand squeezing the blood from my fingers. She was talking and laughing with my daughters through her tears. They were joking about the stupid things I had done over the years to make them laugh during our family nights out. A few of the things I didn't mean to be funny, but I didn't mind as long as they knew that I truly love them.

I couldn't laugh along. It hurt to take a deep breath. I called out to Callie. It was as if someone had sucked all the air out of the room; silence is loud. They all stopped mid-laugh and looked like it was Christmas Day.

"Daddy!" Mikkel was the first to speak, "Didn't you always tell us to expect the unexpected when approached in the dark?" She smiled. "You gotta do better next time, okay?" She kissed my cheek and started crying.

"She'll be alright," my wife chimed in. "She has been here the entire time. We've been battling for the seat by your side every time one of us got up to go to the bathroom." She smiled the smile that made me fall in love with her. "Is there anything I can do for you?"

"Yeah, there is," I answered, gasping between each word.

"What?" They all leaned in.

"Let the blood go back into my fingers!"

———

It took me a while to get my bearings back when I was released from the hospital. I felt like all my strength had been stolen from me. All the rehab and exercise just wasn't making me feel like I used to. The last couple of days, I had only felt up to sitting and watching TV while I let time just run away.

"In today's news, our local DA has dropped charges against the young teenage girls who allegedly attacked three men, who they apparently shot and burned after the men's attempted home invasion."

———

I see a whole new side of my daughters. In all the time that's passed since that terrible night, the concerns that I was worried about have been answered. The problems I thought they couldn't handle have been resolved. For all those years, we had been informing and warning them, and I saw now that they had truly been listening and understanding all the time. I am impressed with them and the way the prophetic Scripture holds true. God is truly amazing. I am alive. My wife and my daughters are stronger than I ever knew. All the reading, praying, and studying has made all of this turn out to be a rewarding experience. Now, after six months, all I have to do is go back to church and give thanks properly.

2
Planting Daisies!

"Run!"

I looked and couldn't see a thing around me.

"Run!" came a loud whisper out of the darkness.

"Run!"

I couldn't hear anything but the sounds of our shoes snapping sticks as they hit the ground. I think I felt the tree before I realized I ran into it. My legs and lower back hurt like hell.

"Get up!" The loud whisper rang in my ears as four hands grabbed me to pull me up.

"Run!"

It's been like this for a while, running nonstop. We don't have a clear direction to go. It's just too dark to be running so hard in woods that are too dense for all this mess. I feel like a child just starting out. I am on wobbly legs. I wanna stop, but if I stop I think it'll be my last time.

"Stop, I hear water!"

We stopped. The sound of rushing water seemed to be shouting at us. The sound of a river is distinct. We walked to the water's edge like deer in headlights. I felt as if I were a deer in headlights. It felt like somebody was watching us.

"Somebody has to watch our backs!" I whispered.

I thought to myself as I scanned over the waters, *I didn't remember it being this big or moving this fast.* We had to be upstate somewhere. The stars were only giving off a small amount of light. It was like the moon was scared of whatever and whoever we were running from. It was too dark to see any good distance away.

"I ain't watching nothing." Joe bent down to drink and buried his face in the water. "Damn, that's good!" He wiped his face in his hands. "We've been running for a long time. I am tired. I ain't a young kid anymore."

"Shhhh!" someone pushed out over all the heavy breathing.

"I ain't doing a damn thing." He turned back towards the woods. "Come on and do your worst, you bitches!"

He turned and bent to drink more. We followed suit. I counted seven. Last I knew, it was ten of us when we started out running. It was just too dark. This was the third time they had let us out. But each time they did, the guys seemed to be acting differently. Some were scared to move. Those're the ones we had to leave behind. Seven of us made it to the water.

I drank. It was so cold. I didn't mind thinking of bears or other animals lurking near this same water. I was just as thirsty as everyone else.

"Don't leave the shallows!" I whispered as loud as I could.

"What?" several of the guys answered back.

"We have to go." I turned to walk out of the water. "If you get totally wet, it will be harder for you to run."

I just hate stupid people. They all ran into the deeper water and dove in.

Thwack! Thwack! Thwack!

It sounded like tree branches breaking. I turned to see several men running towards us. I couldn't make out their faces. I just started to run as I screamed at the others. Were those *gunshots*?

"Let's go!" I didn't hear them leave the water over my own screaming.

My body felt heavy. I couldn't take a full step. I knew that I had fallen, but I didn't feel a thing when I hit the ground. I do remember thinking how big the mosquitoes were. Then everything went black.

—————

"Hi, welcome to the Daisy Retreat."

"Hi." As the door snapped closed behind me, I caught myself flinching and glanced down at my skirt to cover my nervousness. I stole a quick look around the little office and noticed that most of the other women there didn't look as scared as I felt. "I'm Sandra Welbourne. I have an eleven o'clock appointment.

"You're a little bit early." She smiled and pulled out a clipboard with several sheets of paper. "You need to complete only the high-lighted portions and I will have a copy of everything for you to take with you when you leave." She smiled again. "Have a seat over there." The phone interrupted her. "Take your time," she added as she answered the telephone. I stood motionless and waited for her phone conversation to end.

"How long will this interview take?" I asked as soon as she got off the phone.

"Oh, the evaluation takes about a half hour or so. It's nothing to worry about."

"My attorney told me that it would take a while because of your case loads."

"That was months ago. Several of our clients have chosen to go back to school or to work here and assist us on a voluntary basis.

It does help out when the people working with you have been in your shoes."

"I understand."

I sat down and started to write. It hit me all at once. The receptionist had been raped too. Not only had she been raped, but she didn't look like she was worrying about anything.

Ring! Ring! Ring! The phone continued calling out for attention.

I watched as the receptionist began chatting into her headset. She smiled as she talked and answered questions from people around her. Talk about someone on the *joy juice*. I watched the people in the office move about as if everything were fine. I kept asking myself if this place could be real—could all of these women be survivors? How could so many women just get over it? It's been four months and I still can't get the smell of his breath out of my nose. I am still looking over my shoulder every time I get in and out of the car, walk in and out of my apartment, or leave church or any store. It's as if my life just completely stopped because of him.

"Here's the paperwork." I looked into her eyes. They seemed strong and reassuring.

"Okay, have a seat and Monica will be out to get you in a few minutes." She smiled at me again. "Hey, don't worry. Everything will be fine."

"Okay." I didn't feel calmer, just protected by her words and smile.

I caught myself watching the receptionist. She thumbed through the papers and slid them into a purple folder. She put it to the side and went back to answering and smiling into her headset. Ten minutes passed quickly as I watched everyone and flipped through several fitness magazines.

"Sandra?" a thin, muscular black woman asked. "Are you ready to come in?"

I nodded and put the magazine back on the rack.

"I'm Monica Surles. I'll be your counselor for the first phase of your time with us. All those feelings that have been beating you down for the past weeks and months will go away. I can assure you of that . . ."

She smiled and opened the door to her office. It was nicely decorated. I guessed were her family members. Looking around, I noticed that the space was filled with plants, pictures of her, and people. I sat down while she continued on with her welcome speech.

" . . . and nothing in this world will stop us from getting you back either to your old self, or even stronger than you've ever felt in your life. No one has the right to put their hands on another person to take what is not freely given.

"We are called the Daisy Retreat because we believe that in order to overcome all that we have been through, we must first leave our old world behind and return stronger, smarter, defiant, and not the least bit scared of walking out of our homes at any time of the day or night."

As she kept talking, I fiddled with my little can of mace, which now has a permanent place on my keychain.

"We have all been through the same pains and trials as you have. Not one counselor here will just tell you that they '*feel your pain*' without knowing exactly what you are feeling. This is not just going to be the old, 'Come in and cry and bawl about how devastated your life has become because of the actions of some low-life.' We will help you through a planned way of getting over and away from the memory and hurt that has taken place.

"We will go with you to every court appointment. You are not alone in this any longer. Before you leave today, I'll give you the numbers of four other counselors that will be open to answer your calls anytime."

"Four counselors?" I had to ask, "This isn't a one-on-one type of assistance facility?"

"We want you to be and feel safe with us. No one outside these walls will know what we discuss and do. Remember, there is strength in numbers."

"I am trying to figure out how all of this is going to work. My attorney told me this would be the best place for me to get help."

"And she should know."

"She came through here?"

"Yes and no," she continued to explain, "Daisy Retreats are in three countries and twenty-nine states. She received assistance a while ago in another state." My ears perked up. "If you want details, you will have to get them from her. It is not my place to speak of her time."

"I understand." I actually did, but I just wanted to know how I could hope to come out of this—I wanted to put a real face to the fact that I am not the only one that this has happened to.

Our conversation lasted for over an hour. I watched a video that showed a weeklong retreat, including exercise classes, swimming, and small speeches from others who have made it to the other side. Monica is one of those people that you feel that you can immediately open up to. I told her things about my attack that had kept me buried under guilt. After I had released all of that, I felt the pressures melt off my shoulders. The walk out of the offices felt nothing like when I entered. The video, the explanation of why Daisy Retreat exists, and knowing that I am not alone made me want to return. I felt good, but I knew that I'd never walk anywhere without looking at everyone suspiciously. I didn't think I would ever be able to let that go.

I got to my car and heard someone coming towards me. My heart stuttered for a second as I fumbled to turn my keys over to my pepper spray. I held tight and turned.

"Sandra!" It was Monica. "Wait!"

I let out a smile. It was a relief.

"You forgot the phone numbers. You have to keep in contact with us," she said as she smiled. "Call any one of us from now on, okay?" I nodded. "We can't stand through this alone." She smiled as she handed me the three-by-five card. "Okay?"

"Okay." I took the card and looked at it for a few seconds. "I'll call you tomorrow."

"No, you'll call me when you make it home." She looked into my eyes. "I want to know that you are doing okay and that you've made it home safe," she told me, smiling, "I still call my four contacts twice a week. And it's been over seven years since I came through Daisy."

"Okay, I'll call you in about an hour." She looked skeptical. "I *will* call. I have no one else in this town that I can talk to right now."

"Remember Sandra, you have a support system that has been in place for well over forty years." She turned and left, calling over her shoulder, "I'll be waiting for that call."

I got into my car and put the three-by-five on the passenger seat next to my purse—but only after I looked into the backseat. I turned on the radio as I drove off. It was the first time that I had wanted to hear anything but silence. I had told myself that if it was off, I would be able to hear if someone was in the car with me. I felt comfortable. On the drive home, I took in the sunset over the surrounding buildings. I drove a few miles under the speed limit. I saw that they'd changed the marquee at Rosaria's Flower Shop. I couldn't remember when they replaced the old one. It had to be in the past four months, because I had been in there twice since my attack.

"That thought just scared me," I said aloud to myself.

I took a couple of deep breaths when I stopped at the red light on Eldorado and Blossom. My thoughts went back to their old routine. *Two blocks*, I reminded myself. Just two more blocks and I'd be at my apartment complex. My slow driving allowed me to notice several burned-out streetlights. I made a mental note to call the city in the morning; I would tell them exactly which ones to replace. I got to the gate and turned in.

"Dang, the gate is still open." I still found myself talking out loud. The gate had been in the same condition since I moved into this complex three months ago. I scanned the parking lot for stray people and the lazy security guy who was never at his guard's station—probably out trying to chase some tail. "Damn rent-a-cop."

I slowed to pull into my parking spot, but there was a car already there. I stopped to look for an open, well-lit spot. The only spot that was free was directly under a light that I knew had been working last night.

"That's too far, and it's getting way too dark," I said to myself as I backed up to the car that was parked in my spot. I wrote down the license plate number. The manager would hear about this and the security guard in the morning. I put my pen and paper down and looked back to the dark parking spot. I stared harder than I did when I noticed the empty spot. I could swear I was looking at someone standing by the wooden fence that lined the property.

"Oh, hell no!" I said as I backed out of the parking lot and turned around at the guard's station. "Somebody was in the car that was in my damned parking spot!"

I flipped my cell open and pressed seven. I had my lawyer's number there. I looked in the mirrors. The car that was parked was now headed out of the parking lot behind me. I made two lefts. The car made the same lefts. I pressed the hands-free button.

Ring! Ring!

I took a right. I turned left to turn right over on Dunbar Street. I saw no one. *No one was on the street at six-fifteen?* The car appeared again.

Ring!

"Hello?" she finally answered.

"Finally!"

"Sandra? Where are you?"

"I just turned on Dunbar."

"What?" Questions at a time like this. "Why?"

"Tameka, I know it's him. He has someone with him." The tires squealed as I made a left on Madison. "He was at my apartment complex. How did he find me?"

"Who are we talking about?" More questions at the wrong time. "Are we talking about Joe Pickens?"

"Girl, stop asking me questions and tell me something to do."

"You know the Starbucks on Garth?"

"Who in the hell doesn't?" As I spoke, I wondered why she would send me there. People—stupid. "I think it's about four blocks west of me."

"Go there. I'm callin' the cops." She paused for a second before adding, "I'll call you back."

"Okay."

"Hey, don't speed."

"What?"

"I want them to catch him in the act." I slowed to the speed limit and made a right. "Tell me what kind of car he's in."

My heart was beating so fast that I hadn't noticed that there was rain falling. I gave her the information on the car and the plates. I hung up the telephone and waited for her to call me back. I stopped at the red light across from the Starbucks. The car pulled up behind me. I watched in the mirror as they shouted at each other. The light seemed to take forever. Like it was on the side of evil. The light in that car came on and my mouth went dry.

Ya gotta have faith. Da faith. Da faith. Da faith.

The sound of my ringtone startled me. "Hello?"

"Sandra, there should be two cars on you right now."

"I don't see any." As I looked around, two dark Crown Vics pulled up. "Wait, they're here!" One was pulling into the lane behind them and the other alongside them.

The two men darted from the car. Both were followed by a police officer. I heard the sound of sirens start and stop.

"Are you okay?" The right question.

"Yes. Yes I am." My hands were shaking. "I am still scared though."

"I know you are." Tameka sounded like she'd been there too many times. "Pull into the parking lot. I'll be there in a couple of minutes."

I pulled in and parked by a small black car. The tint was too dark to see in. As I turned the engine off and opened my door to get out, the door of the black car opened as quickly as mine.

"Sandra, are you alright?"

"Monica?" I was shocked. "Did you just pull up here?"

"Yes, we did." A short, well-built woman exited the driver's side. "Let's go inside and get out of this mist."

As we walked, I got an uneasy feeling.

"How did you know to meet me here?" I asked. Had they been following me too?

"Tameka called everybody," Monica answered as she opened the door to the café and stepped inside. She pointed to a table. "I told you that you are not alone in this any longer."

"I believe you now." I felt relieved to know that Joe Pickens would be back in jail for a long time. "But how did the police get here so quick?"

"Would you believe that several of them have had the same problem that we have?" She smiled. "So we are always in contact with each other. They're on an undercover squad. That's why they were in the area. There are others who feel our pain and assist us from time to time." She motioned to the woman. "This is Carron. She is a police officer and will get some information from you. Okay?" My uneasiness left.

"Okay." I had a question. So I went ahead and asked, "You are telling me that you guys are really connected, right?"

"Wait until Tameka gets here." Carron spoke, "It'll take a while to explain why we are so well connected."

"Oh dang! Oh dang!" As I opened my eyes and licked my lips, I felt the stubble of my beard and remembered how the cops laid in to me when they put on the cuffs. I couldn't move my legs. "Joe?" He didn't move. "Joe?!"

I tried to reach out my arm to shake him, but I couldn't feel my arms. "Joe, are you alive?"

"Man, shut the hell up." He didn't open his eyes.

"What?" I asked him a stupid question, "Man, why we tied up like animals?"

"It's those cops," Joe answered without opening his eyes. "They took us somewhere. I don't think we're gonna see a cell anytime soon."

"I should've followed my first mind and not went out with you after that darn girl." I was pissed. "Every time I'm with you I get screwed."

"Randy," he called to me in a low voice. "Randy."

"What?" I was wishing that I wasn't tied up so I could punch him in the face. "What in the world could you tell me right now?"

"Don't say another daggum word."

"Daggum word!" I yelled, "Daggum word! Daggum word!"

"Boy, shut the hell up!" he shouted over my ranting, "You giving them too much information." He took a deep breath between insults. "Dumb ass!"

"I'm tied up. You're tied up! I just know that I'ma die because of your lying, cheating, stealing, raping tail."

"Boy, I oughta . . . "

"You oughta what? Spit on me?" I laughed. It felt crazy good. "That's all you will be able to do. We'll be on lock down, dummy!"

"Hey!" A voice came from the corner, "You dumb asses seriously need to shut up."

"Who the hell are you?" Joe always thinks he can whip the heck out of any body.

"They're recording every word we say." The voice had a Hispanic twang to it. "How do you think we all got here in the first place?"

"Whoever it is better start talking and do some untying." Joe clearly still wanted to be in charge.

"Ya'll don't get it," came another voice from behind me. I couldn't really make out how big the room actually was because the lighting was dim. "We've broken the law and these guys are taking guys like us from the face of the earth."

"I ain't done nothing but hang out with this fool of a cousin." I got scared. I couldn't move my body at all. My head was swimming. "I ain't done one thing wrong."

"Randy, shut the hell up!" Joe still wanted to be in charge.

"Joe, I ain't scared of you. You shut up. I'll tell you guys everything I know on this jerk." I talked over his shouting at me, "Video tape me! Record me! I ain't going down with him again."

"Randy, shut the hell up!" As if Joe pushing the base in his voice would make any difference. "Man, they ain't killing nobody up in here. People will be looking for us." He paused for a second. "I can tell you that much is true. Someone will be looking for me."

"Who?" I couldn't think of anyone. "Who's gonna look for us? Neither one of us got good jobs. We're ex-cons. We're both sorry-ass fathers. I ain't called my T-Jones in seven months. Who in the world is gonna miss us? Answer me that, Joseph?"

"Let a couple of days pass," he said, smugly. "I have to be in court on Tuesday for that bogus rape case. They'll be looking for me."

"Yo dude!" a black voice rang out from the other side of the room. "It's Friday and you've been in here for a week . . . sleeping."

The place erupted in laughter. It was so loud and strong my heart dropped.

"Shut up! This mess is not funny at all," Joe insisted. They kept on laughing.

"Better shut up and watch the little television they let us have before they put us back to sleep."

"I ain't worried about none of you stupid bums," Joe said, getting in his insult.

"Joe, you are the stupidest rapist in the world." I had to add my two cents in. If I were being recorded, I wanted them to know that I wasn't involved. "You are the one that stalks and beat women to get a nut."

"Get that mess right," he shouted at me to get over the others still talking and laughing about Joe's snoring and talking in his sleep. "I don't beat them bitches. I bang the hell out of 'em. They all enjoy every moment of this nine-and-a-half inches.

"Oh, big man thinks he's packing a pipe!" one of the guys shouted, and the laughter broke out again.

"I measured my joint. I know it's real." Joe just kept burying himself deeper. "That last 'ho was asking for it. Always primping by the mailboxes and swishing that ass at me. I know she enjoyed it. The bitch had an orgasm while I was banging the hell out of her."

"You think that that was something good?" I hate his funky tail. "Taking something that's not yours. You are a piece of crap." I hate his sorry tail. "And to think that I actually got into a car with you. I called you cousin all my life. Loved you like a brother. Man, somebody oughta cut off your nine-inch Johnson.

"Hell, that's just childish." Joe was still running his mouth, "Ain't nobody cutting nothing. I'll tell you what's gonna happen: I'll go to jail. I'll get out. I'll move to another city and find me a fat bitch to marry and bang for the rest of my life." He chuckled, "It's only right. I sowed my oats and I am ready to be a good citizen."

"Good citizen?" The voice came from the guy in the corner, "Man, I think that this room and the drugs have taken your mind. You ain't getting out of here alive."

"I don't care what any of you bums say." Joe always stayed cocky. "I know that these clowns will let us go, and all things will fall in line. They have done it for me for the past ten years. My luck has always been good in bad situations. It'll come through for me again."

"No, it's not." The voice came again, "I know I been in and out of here for at least six months. They move us and feed us and run the hell out of us. Many have come and gone. All of us have been in this building for more than three months at least."

"All of who?" This should have been my first question. "How many people are in here?"

"People? Dude, it's just men in here."

"It used to be twelve. That was weeks ago," the Hispanic voice said, "It's nine of us now."

"I think it should be back up to ten." An unclear voice came from behind me, "Hey, Ronald?"

"Ronald?" several of the guys called out, over and over.

"It's nine of us," he said after a few seconds of silence, "Ron's gone."

No one said a word for a few minutes. I got groggy and couldn't hold my eyes open for too long. I could have sworn that I saw a few people moving around us. Or maybe I was wishing it someone was coming to release us from our bonds. When I did wake, I was in this small-ass room and in some red boxers. My thighs and nuts were hurting like hell. It hurt to stand up or move my legs. I felt weak all over. You know, kind of like I hadn't been doing nothing but sleeping a drunk off. My body felt whipped. I sat in the corner and took the bandage off my forearm and inspected the large bruise underneath.

I reached down to take a whiz in this square-looking toilet. All I could do was scream. My package hurt like hell. Pissing was a treacherous chore. It seemed to take all of five minutes to dribble out past the pain. My balls were swollen. I started thinking that these people had injected me with something or beat me while I was out. I just hurt. And I was hungry.

Click! Click! Click! The sounds came from the left wall.

I moved to the opposite side of the room. I wanted to try and take at least one of the bastards holding me in this small-ass room down.

Click. Thwap—Boom!

Planting Daisies

I was shaking and I didn't know why. A door opened. It was at the bottom of the wall, probably two feet wide. Too small for me to slide through. A brown box came through and the small door closed as fast as it had opened. I opened the box. I was hoping it was some clothes because I was cold as hell. It was food. There were two bologna sandwiches, five Oreos, some Fritos—all of it crammed in a sandwich bag. I ate it all. The bread was dry and didn't have any spread on it, but the thought did cross my mind that I might be eating my last meal.

After eating, I walked around the little room looking for anything that could let me know whether they were watching me. A small flaw in the paint or in the metal that covered the walls might allow me to think of a plan to get the hell out of there. After a few minutes of inspection, I sat in the corner and stared at the small toilet, thinking of the training toilet that I had purchased for my niece. I sat there and I rubbed my sore balls.

"It's cold in here!" I shouted, hoping someone would answer. No one did, and I fell asleep after a long while of silence.

"Randy!" a voice came through the speaker mounted on the unreachable ceiling.

"Randy!" it shouted again. The ceiling had to be at least nine feet high.

"Randy!" I stood and almost fell. "A door will open in thirty seconds. You will go through the door and follow the lights. Do not try to detour. Punishment is a finality."

There was a long silence.

Click! Click! Click! The sound came through the wall.

"Hey!" I shouted as I stood, "I will not participate in this mess!"

Click! Click! Click! It must be a series of locks. That's what I figured.

"Randy!" the voice came into the room, but this time it was a lot louder, "Do not detour. You will not see your Bowser again."

"My dog?" I was startled for a second. "You bastards got my dog too?"

Click! Click . . . Shaaaaaboom! The door opened hard. Phwam!

I started to run through the door. Fear had a stranglehold on my legs and I could hardly stand as I thought about my dog being done in. Besides, my nuts still hurt like hell.

"Leave my dog alone." All this mess was because of Joe. Always making me lose all my stuff. "I ain't hurt nobody!" I yelled, "Why don't y'all let me go home?!" There was no answer.

I tried walking fast down the hallway. The lights above me would go out as soon as one farther ahead would come on. I tried to look around, but the only light available was always the one just ahead of me. I tried to touch the wall. It was cold and hard, just like the room I'd left. I heard water running. It kept getting louder as I kept walking closer.

As I got to the end of the dark hallway, lights came on and blinded me for a few seconds.

"Step into the shower and put the clothes on that have been provided," the disembodied voice commanded.

I looked at the little bench on the left of the door. There sat a pile of folded clothes and a pair of white-and-black tennis shoes. I stepped into the running water before I dropped my underwear on the shower floor. The water felt so good to my aching body. My arms, back, and hips were all taking in the soothing flow of the water. The soap only added to my awakening realization that I'd been screwing up my entire life and needed to change my behavior before I really ended up dead or worse.

The water shut off. I took that as my cue to dry off and get dressed. I liked the jogging pants and T-shirt. All of it was Nike. I felt like I was an important jock. I put the socks and tennis on. The entire outfit was just cool as hell. I couldn't afford any of it any time over the past four years. I felt like the shiznit.

Click! Click! Click! The noise of an opening door put me on the alert. *Shaaaaaboom!*

A door opened on the other side of the shower and I went through it. It was just another room. As I glanced around, I felt a sharp pain across the entire back of my head. Darkness overtook me.

"Hey Sandra, how ya doing today?" The office wasn't as full as it usually was this time of the week.

"I'm okay, Michelle. I'm just tired from last night's training class."

"Girl, I know. They are intense workouts, but they're worth it." She smiled and turned to answer the telephone.

I walked over and took a seat in the same chair that I'd sat in before my last four counseling sessions. Two months of talking and physical training had helped me cope with all the changes I'd had to make since all this mess began. I'd been working on not allowing the memory of his touch to tear through my mind like it had so many times before. It's almost like I would have unleashed a demon if I thought on him too long. I still shook sometimes at night at the thought of having the nightmares begin again.

"Hey Sandra!" Michelle called me to come back and talk, "The phone hasn't really been ringing that much today since everyone is gone on the retreat."

"The retreat?" I had heard about the outings the clients often participated in. No one had ever told me where they went. They all just said they always have the best of times. "They'll be gone for how long—a week?"

"Naw, just four days and three nights." She knew I was still curious.

"Is that where Jamie, Lori, and Callie went this week?" All ladies I had met in class.

"I think so." She looked at the large calendar on her desk. "Callie usually passes on the summer retreats." I looked at the single light flashing on the telephone. "Hold up one minute," she told me.

She answered the telephone as I turned to see Monica walk out of her office with two well-dressed men. She motioned for me as the men left the building.

"Hey, how are you doing?" she asked, smiling at me. "Come on in. We need to talk about a few things."

My heart dropped as I felt a chill crawl up my back. I couldn't get any words to leave my lips. My mouth had become too dry. I just sat down and put my purse against my stomach as I prepared myself for bad news. I felt the pounding of my heart with every breath.

"Sandra, girl, don't be frightened. I have some news for you—some of it good, some of it bad. But after I tell you, you can't utter a word to any living soul."

"Okay, I won't," I answered, anxious to hear the news.

"Joe Pickens has disappeared." She sat on the corner of her desk. "The gentlemen who just left were detectives. They told me they put out a fugitive warrant for his arrest a couple of weeks ago."

"A couple of weeks ago?" I moved to stand up. "What do I need to do?" Despite all my self-defense exercises, my legs didn't have the strength to lift me.

"You don't have to do anything. He's been out-of-pocket for almost nine weeks now"

"Nine weeks?" I was scared.

"He won't be bothering you again." She smiled, as if it would comfort me. "I can assure you that he won't."

I could tell by the look in her eyes that she knew a great deal more than she was letting on.

"How can you be so confident that he won't bother me again?"

She stood up, walked to the back of the desk, and opened a drawer in one of the filing cabinets that held several pictures of women I had seen in training classes.

"I know because of this."

She slammed a jar on her desk. It was the size of a small mason jar. There was a small, dark object floating in it.

"What the hell is that?" It looked like a piece of burnt Italian sausage.

"That, my dear, is the two-and-a-half inches of Mr. Joseph Picken's pecker." She smiled one of the harshest smiles that I had ever seen.

"Oh, damn!" I was in shock, but all I could do was stare at the small jar in front of me. Rotten, stinking, rapist bastard finally got his. Then it hit me. "How in the world could you do that? Where is he?" I looked into her eyes. I saw no fear. "Is he still alive?" What I saw in her eyes looked like satisfaction.

"He is alive." She smiled. "In about six hours he'll be running for his life."

I was satisfied. I don't know why I wanted to give him any compassion; he didn't have any when he punched me in the face. Screw him.

"Do you mean he'll be picked up by the police?"

"Eventually." She sat down in her chair. "He'll be put down where he can't run from anyone anymore.

I found myself scared for a new reason. What kind of camp was I in?

"Isn't that kidnapping?" My voice cracked, "Can we go to jail for this?"

"Go to jail? Girl, no. We didn't *technically* take him anywhere. And he'd have a hell of a time proving it, much less that you knew anything about it." She picked up her phone. "Can you come in here for a few minutes?" She hung up the phone and looked at me as if her stare could calm my nerves. "Sandra, you haven't a thing to worry about."

My sympathy should have been just for me and the six other women he had taken advantage of.

The door opened and in walked two women. They were so familiar that I knew I should know their names. I recalled that the first woman was the judge on my case, but I couldn't place the second woman to save my life. But my instincts told me I should know who she was. She spoke first.

"Sandra, I am Dianne Reynolds. I was the nurse you talked with the night that you were attacked and hospitalized."

"I knew that I'd met you before! I just couldn't put a name to the face." I was filled with questions. "Thank you for talking with me. I know it wasn't a part of your job."

"That's okay. I think I need to—we need to tell you a story that will shed a little light on why we're here. It will give you some answers to how this place operates and why we've been working you so hard in the exercise classes and at the gun range.

"Our beginnings," Dianne explained, "have a great deal to do with why we make such a point of keeping in touch with one another. Not only here in Baytown, but in a number of cities throughout this country and several others.

"Let me begin by telling you that in 1964," Dianne continued, "there was a woman named Daisy Reynolds who was raped and beaten by several of her high school classmates. She was left in an old building to bleed out and die. This building stands in the same place—the cornerstone was laid over the exact same location as the original. She was found a day after her attack by three white girls: the younger sisters of the boys that committed her rape. The rest is the beginning of our history."

No one said a word. I felt motionless as if I were looking into the past. The judge seated herself in the chair next to me. Monica sat behind her desk, looking for my reaction, while Dianne leaned against the wall as she went on.

"The story goes that the three girls overheard their brothers bragging about what they had done to their black classmate and how she deserved it for walking in the wrong part of town. These girls took Daisy home and explained to her family what had happened. Weeks after the attack, the four girls became close friends despite their brothers' actions. Their friendship became our beginning. Their number grew to ten after the same boys decided to take several other victims, the last being a white girl. They were arrested for that crime. They each only spent one year in jail for her rape, with no time for their crimes against the black girls. Most say it was because the boys were sixteen and seventeen at the time. These ten little girls wrote furious letters to the newspaper and even visited the mayor and the District Attorney's office on a weekly basis. Nothing was ever done. It was the sixties, so it was just another thing to sweep under the rug in a town run by the good ol' boy program.

"By the time the boys had gotten out jail, Daisy had taken her own life. The group had grown to twenty-two angry girls. They were angry because they had lost their friend, and because the justice system had never recognized that the flower that had been stolen from them could never be replaced by a year or two behind bars."

Dianne stopped and reached for the pitcher of water that was on Monica's desk. The judge took the opportunity to put in her spin on the story.

"By this time, the friendship of the girls had grown so strong that the color lines between them were broken. They all had suffered the same fate and wanted to repay their attackers by any means that they could. They all made a pact, the same words we recite before we begin each exercise class, group counseling session, aerobic workout, self-defense class, or gun training class."

As she spoke, I found myself repeating it again in my head: *We will not stand broken and defeated. We will plant our roots deeper. Our petals shall be stronger than they were before. We shall overcome by planting daisies and sowing new seeds to reap the bountiful harvest.*

"I know the pledge, but what happened to the boys after they were released from jail?"

She continued the story with a clear and steady voice, ignoring my question as if to say I should wait for the answer to reveal itself to me. She spoke as if she had repeated this same story a thousand times before.

"The boys thought they were free and clear. Three of the boys and their families moved out of state within weeks of their release. They said that the city had too many bad influences and they all had to move so their sons could have good futures.

"Every time I tell this, it's as if those girls are being raped all over again. It's like I'm being chased down in my dorm room again. It angers me to that they could just move on and not have to suffer for what they've done. They all can restart and move on without having to remember the pain they caused and all the people they've hurt. Their move didn't give Daisy a better future."

She stopped and took a breath. No one said a word. I think we could all relate to the way she felt.

"Anyway, the boys went about their lives. The girls, well, they met in secret for weeks. They talked about their mistreatments at the hands of those boys, uncles, brothers, and cousins. They planned a system for retribution. It took a little over fourteen years. They all carried on with their lives. Some went to college, some got married, and others started work. They still stayed in touch, continuing to meet in secret.

"As the fourteenth year came to a close, the purchase of the building and property was their Christmas present to Daisy. They had the building torn down and this building put up in its place. They started the first counseling center for women in the county."

"Are those the women in the picture hanging above the entrance?" I had been wondering who those women might be and why they were there for the longest time.

"Yes, that's all of them. That picture was taken two weeks after they opened the doors. The jar that you see in front of you is a result of their planning, patience, and fortitude.

"It took them three years to track down the all those boys. It was brutal at first. It took a while to master the art of giving back what they had received. The first two only lost one testicle, but each spent several weeks in the hospital with infections. The others . . . Well, they were totally castrated and left to suffer as Daisy had suffered.

"I can't go into the details of the wheres, whys, and hows of this place. All I can tell you is that all of those involved work in every facet of life. We have mothers, police officers, judges, pilots, dockworkers, travel agents, lawyers, teachers, and a great many in local and federal governments in this country and several others. We have been fine-tuned and revamped. There are twenty-six Daisy Retreats in the US, Canada, and Mexico: all of them working toward the same goal. This is why we hold our retreats twice a year. Retributions have to be planned and carried out without too many errors."

I looked around the room as another question came to mind. It was a lot to take in.

"How do you know that I won't tell the police?" I knew the answer as soon as I finished asking.

Monica answered just as quickly, "How will you know that you're not talking to one of us?" She smiled and went on, "As she just told you, we are everywhere. We are not just women. There are men who've suffered the same fate and some that are just sympathetic to the cause and would like to right a tremendous wrong. A few from this area have tried and report us. They've reported us, and then they had to relocate to another part of the country because they couldn't find a job in the state. This is too important to have fall apart because of someone else's stupidity. Too many lives are at stake. Too many what-ifs and what-could-have-beens. Rapists only become murderers in the long run. We stop that cycle."

"Hell, I am not telling a soul. Joe Pickens got what he deserves. He needs to be somebody's bitch in prison." I took a deep breath to ask, "When can I go on a retreat?"

"You need more training in Combat Martial Arts before you can travel with anyone, but it's in your future." They smiled and passed the jar around, laughing, "His ass is gonna be in for a Floridian surprise."

———

I think I dozed off again. I opened my eyes to someone shaking me.

"Man, come on!" He kept shaking me. "We got to get out of here as soon as we can."

He pulled my arms and made me get to my feet. My knees felt so strange. I thought about just laying back down, but the urgency in his voice let me know that something was seriously about to happen. I couldn't see a thing in front of me. I heard what I thought might be screams in the distance, so I didn't look. I just kept on running. It felt like some type of dream I was trapped in, but I knew that it was all too real.

We had made it to the river, but as I tried to run back for shore, all I felt was the ground taking a good blow to my face. When I was able to open my eyes, I saw several figures dressed in black. My hands weren't tied, so I figured the best thing to do was take one on and find out what they planned on doing with me. That was a mistake.

"Grab his monkey ass!" came a scream from behind me.

———

I thought what I had heard was a woman's voice, but the ass-whipping I'd gotten didn't match up. I was hit with more kicks and punches than I thought could be thrown by any living being. It had been more than a week now, and my face was still hurting beyond imagining.

"So what do you want us to do?" the detective at the desk asked.

"I want to make a report of my kidnapping and attack."

"Okay, you told me that you don't remember what day you were taken, where you were taken from, or how long you think you were gone." He just looked at me as if I were drunk or high. "I can take the report and submit it to my captain, but I don't for the life of me know where to start. You don't even live in this city."

"What?" I asked because I had never left Baytown to go anywhere. "What are you talking about?"

"Let's see . . . " He tapped away on the keyboard for a few minutes and printed out several pieces of paper. "Your name is Randy Love. You were born outside of Houston. You've been arrested several times for theft, burglary, and attempted kidnapping. You have been released on parole from Texas to here in Des Moines, Iowa. And now you come in here with an outrageous story that you've been kidnapped and beaten by some women in the woods. The woods that you can't remember the location of, plus you've got this dog tied to your wrist."

I looked down and Bowser was staring back up at me. I was still so groggy. I'd thought the pinch on my arm was handcuffs.

"I don't know what else to tell you," I took a breath before going on, "All I can tell you is that my nuts hurt like hell and I think one is missing."

"Well, I am not touching your balls." The detective leaned back in his chair. "I see here that you are supposed to report to your parole officer on the fourth floor. I think you best get a move on up there and leave the fantasy life for your AA meetings."

I got up and walked to the door. I took a glance at the television that sat in the corner. I saw Joe Pickens in cuffs somewhere in Florida screaming and crying. *That's his ass*, I thought as I touched my pocket and pulled out a set of keys that had an address and apartment number taped to it. These people relocated me. I'm calling my momma and I'ma tell her that I am not going back anytime soon.

Consider This on This Day

Becoming the *Superwoman* You Should Be

In the search for a good life, we sometimes tend to sell ourselves short of all the talents we are given. In particular, women are given a tower of strength, which has all too often been pushed down to what she may wear, how it fits on her, what size she may be, and whether she is sexy enough to be on a guy's arm (if he even takes her out).

God has made a woman to be the "helpmeet" of the man he has created for her. The problem in becoming that *superwoman* . . . Some settle for the first thing breathing and feel angry, upset, disappointed, discouraged, disgusted, and empty at the end of most days. And then there are long days of not believing in their talents or whether they have reached their true purpose and potential.

The fact of the matter is this: *It is more than okay to be single for a while.* There is not a man on this earth worth the salt in your tears if he is not willing to lift you up on a daily basis, thank you for listening to him cry on the bad days that make him want to give up, and appreciate that you are his backbone.

There is not any one person who should rule over how *you* believe and think about yourself. Your self-worth is in the hands of God, and you have been blessed before you realize what you have or who you truly are . . . You do not need one single person to validate what has already been ordained from above. *You* were created to do super things through tough and trying times.

Some would-be psychologists wrongly insist that women are too emotional and cannot handle stressful situations well enough to keep their self-esteem and self-efficacy intact . . . Spit on that and keep pushing on as you have been doing.

To solidify your daily strength, read Psalm 40 and 43. Grace and favor are waiting for you, as well as the hope that we all have in knowing that God will not leave us in a void of unprofitable situations or heated circumstances. It is your choice whether to be the "wifey" or the *superwoman* . . . Choose this day to become who you truly want to remain and be known as.

Ladies, Proverbs 31 speaks of the woman that is behind the man. The Word shows how strong her character is and who benefits from her being that strong rock and tower for her husband.

In being the backbone of that man, your actions cannot mirror his or cause him to stumble and fall. If you are his and he is truly acting as yours, be his by talking openly with him (not to him) and telling him those things that you wish to achieve and how you want to be treated. Mutual respect and true honor for one another can only come when you both clear the air in your household by talking openly and honestly together. And all things confided in each other have to remain between the two of you.

Remember this: He cannot be great unless you are there to help him overcome his shortcomings and failures. *No man* is an island.

But if you are single, love yourself and learn of yourself before meeting that new person. It is okay to be single in a world of broken and barely-working relationships and half-promised or half-married couples. Be true to you and believe in all the things that have been given you by God.

3

Dominoes . . .
Best Laid Plans

I GOT OFF WORK EARLY. I STOPPED AT THE STORE TO PICK UP POP-pa's Seaport coffee and peppermints. It's just one of the things I do every week before I spend some time with him. He has been so happy that I landed the job at the Child Protective Services office; I think it's because he can call me anytime. Most times it's just to talk.

Ring! Ring! Ring! This is the third time I've called his house today without an answer.

"Hi and hello. This is Mr. Willie Johnson. Please leave me a message and I will get back to you at your earliest convenience. Thank you . . . *Beep!*"

I hung up and called back twice with no success.

I have told him time and time again to correct his message. He thinks it's funny to have people tell him that his message has a mistake in it. It gives him something else to talk on the telephone about. But then again, you know how people are when they get up in age and they are alone. Alone . . .

Ring! Ring! I called his neighbor across the street.

"Hello?"

"Hey T-Nanny, it's Toney. How are you?"

34

"I'm okay. I've been baking all morning for the Easter bake sale. How are you doing?"

"I'm on my way to Poppa's and I am not getting an answer. Have you heard from him today?"

"Yes, but that was this morning. He said that he was going to clean up a little and get ready to make some fig preserves for you to give to Paris. Matter of fact, how is she? Y'all serious yet?'

"Uh, no. We're just friends." She and Poppa have been trying to marry us for the longest time. "Do you have time to go over and see if he is still picking figs? I'm about twenty-five minutes out from you."

I heard the clang of pans.

"That's no problem. I have to turn off my oven, but I'll call you back in a few minutes. Let me go put my shoes on."

"Thank you."

My heart was racing. My mind circled around the fact that he was on new blood pressure meds lately. The doctor did say he had been stuck on dueling meds from his last doctor and that it was overwhelming his system. He would sometimes go to sleep and be slow and groggy for days at a time. And on the other hand, I knew he was cutting his pills to save on money. I had been trying to help him with the cost, but in his hard-headedness he kept telling me my money is for me. I love him too much to worry about money.

"*I said a hip, hop, hippy to the . . .* "

"Hello?"

"Toney!" All I could hear was the scream of the smoke alarm. "Toney, you have to hurry. I had to come through the back door. There's smoke everywhere. I turned the pot off." My heart dropped. "I turned the pot off, but I don't see him anywhere!"

"I'm a couple of blocks away." I heard the phone hit the table. She didn't hang up.

"Hello, this is your 911 operator."

"Hello, my name is Toney Marks and I'm on my way to my grandfather's house on 1380 Bradley Street and I'm not getting an answer and there is smoke all through his house!"

"How do you know there is smoke in his house?"

"A neighbor just called me. She's frantically looking for him."

"You said 1380 Bradley Street, correct?"

"Yes, it's the blue and white house in the middle left of the block when you turn off Hemlock."

"Okay sir." She was talking to dang slow. "What happened to your grandfather?"

"I don't know. I just got here. I can hear the smoke alarm."

"Who is that I hear shouting in the background?"

"That's my grandfather's neighbor, T-Nanny."

"T-Nanny? Is that her real name?"

"That's the only name that I have known her by since I was nine years old." I ran in the backdoor and quickly made it to his room. I looked under the bed while the 911 operator was talking to someone else about the location of Poppa's house. "Poppa!" I ran to my old room. "Poppa!" I ran back to the kitchen. I knocked that damned smoked alarm down as I shouted, "Ma'am is someone coming? I don't see him anywhere in here!" I'm losing my cool.

"Sir calm down." As if I could hold onto any part of calm at this point. "Did your neighbor look outside?"

"I don't know. I didn't ask her." I hollered at T-Nanny, who was on the ground looking under the back porch. "Have you looked anywhere else out here?"

"No, I only looked inside first. It's not like him to have a pot on the fire and not be close by."

"She said no. I hear sirens." I felt a small piece of calm when I saw a police officer round the corner of the house into the backyard.

"Okay sir, you can hang up now that the officers have arrived."

We went in all directions; all of us shouting his name. His yard is large. I looked in his old shed and under the bushes that lined the perimeter of the yard. I didn't see anything until I stood and looked across to the fig tree, where I saw officers motioning to come over. I couldn't run fast enough—my legs felt as if they were moving in slow motion. I couldn't get to him fast enough.

He was facedown behind the tree. His little blue bucket was on its side. Several figs had found their way out and were covered by ants. His hands were in fists. They had ants on them. The officer stepped in my way and held me back with his words. Words that cut me deep.

"Do something!" I heard myself screaming as T-Nanny fell to her knees a few feet away. "Get those ants off of him—please!"

Another officer came over to me. He was the largest of the five. How could he tell me it was too late? They didn't even attempt CPR. They didn't even try.

"Can you please move him out of the ants?" They ushered me to the little table we used to play dominoes on.

"Please have a seat here. We'll move him as soon as we can." They walked away without another word.

T-Nanny came over and sat down. I had forgotten about her. We sat and watched as the officers talked, took pictures, and asked questions. We watched as the firemen went in and out of the house, and the neighbors who came and left. They asked more questions about my job, how far away it was and how long T-Nanny had been his neighbor. They even asked me why I broke the smoke alarm. I felt like I was in a bubble with no air.

It took two hours for the coroner's office to show up. His friends came and left in tears. Nothing they could say could make me feel any better. I should have gotten here earlier. Paris came and sat in silence for a while before my family showed up to put on their best demonstration of "distraught love" for a man that they would barely visit. They didn't notice that the ants had gotten to the back of his head and were multiplying by the minute. I wanted to scream. The last time my brother was over here, it was to borrow money that he never intended to repay. Poppa gave it to him anyway.

I watched as they lifted his body. They were not tender in their efforts. They threw his arms across his chest. They dropped his legs as if they were dropping old leaves in a trash bag.

"Why were you not here to help him get those damn figs? You're always here anyway," asked my loving mother, acting as usual. "What the hell happened?"

I took my eyes off the guys in the black coveralls to look at her. "I don't know." My answer came out dry.

"What in the hell do you really know?" Most times she speaks without thinking a great deal about the things she's gonna say. "Did you do something to him so you could get this house after he died? Is that the reason this pale bitch is with you? You two are always

37

thick as thieves." Paris moved to stand. I grabbed her arm to make her stay. "Did you have anything to do with this, you old heifer?" she went on, turning to T-Nanny.

"Margaret, you are overreacting and speaking very ugly to us. I loved your father. Don't come at me like that. I've known him and your mother for fifty-seven years. Grow up and be a woman about this."

"What?" She stepped closer. "I don't know why you think that you can just waltz over here and take what's mine and not be challenged. You are absolutely out of your sorry-ass mind."

"Momma, wait . . . " I tried to step in. She didn't stop talking.

"Wait what? She ain't getting this house or anything else from 'round here." The grin that crossed her face actually looked devilish.

I left the conversation for a second to watch the people circling the fig tree as if they were looking for blood diamonds.

"Mrs. Marks, Mr. Willie just died and you are acting like you have lost your mind." Paris always has to say something, "You are talking about stuff that you had nothing to do with."

"Stuff that neither one of them or you will get your hands on!" Momma started to back away as my brother came over to show his support for her. "Y'all can kiss my butt. I am the only one that is an heir in this yard."

"Toney, don't fuss with Momma over this house. It's hers," my brother put in. Like I said . . . stupid. "Just cuz you got through college and all that, you still ain't no better than me."

"Margaret," T-Nanny spoke as she always has in the past—in a low, strong tone. "I am sixty-four years old. I don't need your dad's things. It's all Toney's. It's been for him before the year your mother went home and my husband died."

Her mouth fell open. I didn't care. Poppa is in somebody's van under a sheet. She was only silent for a minute.

"His? Who the hell says so?" I was still in shock of Poppa going home like that. "Toney, you bamboozled my daddy for his house?" I didn't have a word for her. "You are just like your sorry-ass daddy." She walked off, upset—but not over the death of her own father. "You are as sorry as your thieving daddy!" She kept shouting while my crony brother followed in silence. I was still in a fog.

"It's just emotions making her act like this." Paris was standing with her purse in her hand. "I have to leave." She kissed my forehead, adding, "I'll call you in a little while, okay?"

I nodded. She left. T-Nanny walked away with her. Paris is good people.

After answering more pointless questions about my mother, my brother and his time in and out of jail, the will I did not know a thing about, and how often I spent time with Poppa, I found myself sitting in his rocking chair. The lingering smell of smoke made me mad that I didn't call him during lunch. The photo of us playing dominoes at a church picnic made me want to scream. The silence in the house shouted in my ears and squeezed my chest until tears ran from my eyes.

I got up and tried to clean up the kitchen. I was having trouble walking. I sat on the back steps. No birds were in the trees. I didn't see that old squirrel at the feeder, where he always used to hang. No cars shouted as they skidded over the potholes in the back alley. The silence followed me outside. I walked over to the fig tree and picked up Poppa's old cowboy hat. The leather was old and worn; it reminded me of the feel of his hand the last time we left church together. I still couldn't remember the last time I hugged him.

I sat at the domino table until the stars came out and left again. The fig tree never bowed in sorrow.

T-Nanny came over and brought food. I didn't understand a word that she said. I only heard the Merwin poem, "For the Anniversary of My Death," over and over and over.

I went to the shed. I got the shovel out. I heard the leaves hollering at me as I headed over to dig up the fig tree. I stuck the shovel in the dirt and pulled it out as quickly as I could. The sound I heard reminded me of grandma's wedding ring hitting the dishes as she washed our dinner dishes. Her ring was in the dirt. This was her tree. He planted it for her decades ago.

Damn . . . fig tree.

Now it's mine.

4
Dominoes . . .
Peaches and Apples

"DANG!" BAKER WAS LATE. "I THOUGHT WE'D GET IN ON THE FIRST game.

"Take a seat," Poppa said as he played his first domino, "You know the drill. Stand in line so I can teach you young cats why I put the white dots on black dominoes."

After twenty minutes watching the game, Baker showed up to join us. He sat down next to Bobby, saying nothing.

"Baker, what's up with you?" I had to ask. He was just sitting and smiling. "What've ya done now?"

"Naw, man." He talked through smiling teeth, "I ain't done nothing." He leaned back into the lawn chair. "I met this girl last night at The Main Event and all I have to say is Emu Oil is the thing to have!"

"Man, didn't you just get married?" Jayson chimed in. Jayson had just married Carron last year. "Boy, you are a piece of work."

"No, it wasn't last year." Baker's smile didn't move. "It's been two-and-a-half years now." He paused for a second and put his wedding band back on. "Thank you."

I can't say a thing about him and his actions. All brothers have played on their woman at one time or another.

"Baker, you're gonna get caught," I added my two cents in anyway, knowing he wouldn't listen.

"And you used the Emu Oil for what?" Jayson asked.

"That's what you say." Turning from me, Baker answered Jayson, "The Emu Oil is something I picked up in Longview. I use it for splitting the apple." He stood and patted himself on the butt.

"I was married for forty-six years and never cheated on Agnes." Poppa always tried to bring some sense into our conversations. "And then to talk about the things that should be secret and sacred—boy, you are more than a piece of work. You are becoming a piece of something else."

"Mr. Johnson, no disrespect," Baker said, standing up, "That was a different time and place. Women these days are prepared for two major upsets in their marriages. One is the unexpected baby, and the other is that their good husband will scratch that proverbial itch."

"What?" we all sang out at the same time, sounding like Boyz II Men.

"It's a fact," Baker went on. He really believed all the crap that fell from his pea brain. "Look here, most marriages end in divorce because the first five years are spent trying to be all spiritual and deeply in love." He scanned all of our faces as he talked on, "That's why they fail. To be strong, you've gotta go through a few days of hell to find yourselves some heaven in the house. You have got to find you a freak on the side to better your relationship at home."

"Baker, all marriages have ups and downs." Poppa started talking before Jayson could, "You do something in that manner and you destroy your spiritual connection with that woman. Once you've crossed that line, it will be an uphill battle to get back to her."

"See, that's exactly what I am talking about," Baker retorted, raising his voice like we couldn't hear his stupid tail, "You have to go through some things to make the bedroom relations good.

"Man, shut up and listen," said Bobby. Bobby Blue just found out that he had a son a few years ago. He wanted to get married and all the stuff that goes along with that dream.

Poppa continued and put his dominoes facedown on the table. We all got comfortable to listen.

"It's a connection that has been ordained by God and you are trying to unplug it with stupidity."

"No, sir." Baker talks and talks, "We lived together for nine months before we got married. We did the church thing. The counseling thing. We moved back to the parents' for two weeks before the wedding and didn't have any sexual contact with each other to make the first married night right. So, we were right in the beginning. Besides, I am within my rights. They say that it's normal to get the seven-year itch." He laughed, "I just scratched mine early so it wouldn't become a rash."

Stupid. Just stupid. Just dang stupid.

Slam! Slam! Slam!

The noise came from the front of the house. No one moved, guessing it was probably our neighbor T-Nanny making a racket across the street.

"Boy, who is 'they'?" Jayson asked. "Are 'they' the same people that have been married four or five times and want you to believe that it is okay to keep up the lie of being single while you are married?"

"How the hell do you know?" Baker kept trying to prove his point, "You just got married. And on top of that, that girl can kill you and get away with it." He leaned forward on the chair, adding, "You married a damn cop out of all the women in the world. A cop. That'll keep any brother on the straight."

"Her job is not the reason that I married her, or the reason I live the way I do. I found a woman that fit me in everything."

"Fit you?" he laughed, "Are you living like that?"

"Baker . . . " Poppa was back into the conversation, "Yeah, it's the right word. The woman you should be with fits you in every way: physically, sexually, mentally, and spiritually."

It's no doubt that Jayson has grown up and found what he wanted and needed in his world. He used to be what I call a *Part-Time Player*, but Jayson is a good man and the woman he married just brought it out of him a little more.

"Mr. Johnson, I found the woman I wanted." Baker's explanations were always foul, so I stood by for a load. "She's fine as hell, good-looking, and has a good brain on her shoulders. She fits me sexually. I didn't have to train her too much on that point. We have a good time when we're together. She is mine as I am hers. So, I believe two outside endeavors will not end our relationship in any way. We were friends before we became lovers. Things fit, so we got married."

"That's close, but you get no ribbons for being close to stupid." Poppa pushed his dominoes into the center of the table. "Toney has seen me all of his life." He looked at me and then continued to talk as he looked us over, "The Bible says that *when a man finds a wife, he finds a good thing.* And with any good, God-fearing man, his good thing should be cherished and maintained. Paul said that a man should love his wife as Christ loved the church. And the biggest thing in that for any man is that he be willing to die for his wife on a daily basis."

"Oh yeah," Baker scoffed, "I die for her at least three times a week in the Victorian sense."

He laughed alone.

"Boy, that's not the type of dying he's talking about," I had to chime in between his hahas.

"I know what he's talking about, but it sure does feel good around eleven-thirty at night."

A few chuckles from everyone and the conversation began again.

"I'ma let you into the secret of marital relations. The more the two come together, the better in tune with one another they are." Bobby Blue was right on point as he went on, "The better the communication physically and spiritually, the sounder the house is. That is, as long as the man stays in communication with God."

"Why is everything always put on the shoulders of the man? Don't we have enough to deal with?" He's right and wrong there, I thought. "I just don't get it. If I just happened to run into a honey who's willing to part with the drawers, you're telling me that that'll be some kind of spiritual bomb dropped on my household?"

"Yes, I am, and yes, it is," I answered.

"Toney, no one asked you." He looked at me with some disgust. Like I betrayed him. "You got a girl that has an apple bottom and you're still not even married—yet you're trying to give out advice?" He grabbed a soda out of the cooler. "Just shut up."

"Jazmine has nothing to do with what I am or the way I think. Don't step to me wrong."

"This is just a conversation between men," Poppa interrupted, shutting us down. "All of us are wrong one time or another. Don't start pointing fingers about who has what, who has done this and that, or who has the best-looking woman. I'm trying to give you guys a little knowledge on how to become *good* men and husbands."

"Yeah, yeah," Baker's tone became hard and rude, the way a lot of us do when we realize we are living wrong, "I still say that a stint in the mud helps clear up any muck later on in a marriage." He took a long drink from his soda before adding, "It keeps that woman in line, just knowing that there is another female wanting her man."

The noise from the front of the house was growing louder by the minute. This time there were several voices, all shouting, "Do it!" and "He deserves it!"

"Man, what is going on up front?" Bobby Blue asked as he got up and walked toward the noise. We followed. "Oh, damn!"

"Baker, you really screwed up!" Poppa started laughing and sat on the edge of the porch.

There were two women pouring a ten-pound bag of sugar in his gas tank with a funnel. Three others got in Baker's face and started telling him how sorry a *Keebler* he really was. He should know that when you live in a small town, you can't play two women. There was so much yelling and screaming from Baker and the women who were in front of him, blocking him from stopping the others from taking his tires and pouring more sugar in his gas tank. T-Nanny crossed the street and sat down beside Poppa to chat as they watched.

"Baker, how could you do this to me?" Tacia was crying. Her light brown cheeks were as red as her eyes."

"Girl, I ain't done nothing to you!" Baker had an amazingly deep voice for a white boy. "You know it's just you and me in this world. And here you are with your chicken-headed friends to embarrass me in front my boys. All you had to do was wait at home and we could've talked through this mess."

"You slept with my cousin!" She was mad, not to mention her cussing and screaming friends.

Several neighbors gathered at the corner of the yard. The block was loaded with seniors—there wasn't a great deal of activity around here.

"You had sex with my cousin!" She clenched her fists. "You banged her, Baker! You're a sorry bastard!"

"What cousin, Tacia?"

"The same woman you told last night that she had a good peach basket!" His mouth dropped open. His expression was all the answer she needed. "You told her the same thing you've been telling me for the past four years."

There was a moment of complete silence. Neither of them said a word. It was one of those moments when a conversation could swing in any different direction.

She took a deep breath. She never wiped a tear. "Baker," she said in a low tone, not yelling anymore, "You are a sorry ass bastard."

"Tacia, girl, I love you like I haven't loved anyone else in this world." He reached for her hand. "Baby, we can go home and pray and talk this over." He took a step toward her. "I do confess to you that I hit that girl in the ass, but it didn't mean a thing to me."

"Baker, come here, I just want to show you how much I love you."

He turned and smiled at us. As soon as he turned his head back, though . . . She smacked him with the best left hook I'd seen in my life. His knees buckled like he'd been hit by Lawrence Taylor. Bobby Blue ran over to grab Tacia. I wanted her to hit him again. Her girls stopped their work just long enough to see Baker to hit the ground. They went back to working over his car. Baker struggled to get back to his feet.

Tacia continued to set Baker straight, but from the other side of Bobby Blue's six-foot-four frame.

"When you are able to drive your precious vehicle to the house, then we can pray and talk." She looked at Bobby Blue and then at Baker before adding, "And since you slept with my cousin, you best get your ass checked out. The bitch is dirty."

She turned her face to Bobby Blue. Grabbed both of his shoulders and tongued him down. For a second I wondered if it was the first time the two of them had kissed like that. It just wasn't awkward looking. She walked away, motioning for her friends, who were throwing Baker's tires in the back of a truck. The loaded up and left. Several of the women from the neighborhood just laughed as they gathered at a house across the street and talked. It had to be a good day for them.

"Baker!" Jayson shouted from his seat on the rocking chair on the porch, "Baker, is this the part of the muck that you were talking about?" We laughed. "Want some more Emu Oil?" We laughed harder.

"Baker, boy, you are definitely going to have to do more than pray to get yourself out of this mess." Poppa added his two cents, "But you do know that you are not staying in my house, right?"

Everyone who came to watch the action and play dominoes took a tour around Baker's car, kicked the three empty sugar bags for a laugh, talked about the amount of clothes piled up in his car, and the long, deep scratches and dents that truly showed how a scorned woman reacts to stupidity.

"Bobby Blue, that really wasn't the first time that you kissed that woman, was it?" Poppa could be messy at times. "I only ask 'cause you *definitely* didn't try to hold anything back."

Bobby didn't say a word. He waved as he got into his car and drove off. Baker sat on the steps of the porch in pitiful silence. Me, I followed Jayson and the others to the backyard to start a new game of dominoes and the usual philosophical discussions about neighborhood happenings.

5
Baby Daddy's Blues

I HAD MY FOUR BOXES OF INFORMATION. I HAD BEEN READY FOR this court date for the past five years. I'd grown sick and tired of being pointed at like I don't do the right things in life—sick and tired that all men are sorry and deadbeats. I hated the woman that had my child. She was the sorriest thing that I had ever laid my eyes on. At one time, I thought that she was fine as hell. All she turned out to be was hell.

I didn't know about him for the first four years of his life. It had been an uphill battle to get to know him despite her sorry-ass actions. But I hadn't missed a single payment of child support, and yet all I saw from the money I was always sending to the Attorney General's office was that her hair and nails were done every week.

My son needed me more now than ever.

"Hi," I spoke to the officer who sat in the foyer of the courthouse, "I'm here for a child support court hearing. Can you direct me?"

"Take the elevator up to the third floor and turn left. When you see the long line, sign in and have a seat in the room on the right." He smiled at me, adding, "You're gonna be here for a while."

"Thank you." The word "butthead" came to mind, but I was on a mission.

I got to the third floor and signed in. I sat and thought of nothing else except how I'd been cheated. I'd been cheated out of the best years of my son's life. The amount of money I could've saved is ridiculous, if only I would have known how sorry she would turn out to be. BBD was right when they sang, "Don't trust a big butt and a smile."

It's like I was caught up in that ghetto girl story I read some years back. You know the one. Boy meets girl. Boy is impressed with the package. Future prospects look good. Girl puts on the loving, caring, smart show. Boy sleeps with the girl. They lose the first baby. Boy goes to the service. Girl finds new beau. Girl cheats, says she couldn't wait. Girl wants marriage, a house, and a car right away. Girl wants what she wants. They have goodbye sex. The rest is why I'd ended up in the place I was in right now, singing the Baby Daddy Blues.

I felt played all the way around. I spent four years in the military for nothing. I was prepared to serve her and my country. She had the wrong ideas from the start. Never does any relationship go from zero to one hundred and last. I never promised I could give her the easy life. I wanted her after our second month of dating. The picture she painted for me was done up very, very well. The brushstrokes were seamless. I wish I would have realized then that it was just a faux fantasy.

I waited for my name, Bobby Phillips, to be called. My friends called me Bobby Blue, but I had no friends in court.

"Vivian Minix and Matthew Jones Jr.!" a short white woman called from the doorway, "Vivian Minix and Matthew Jones Jr.?" She looked at her pad and shook her head.

"Ma'am, I'm Matthew Jones." A tall, slender guy stood and walked toward her.

"Sir, if Ms. Minix is not here, you will have to wait until she shows up to see the judge."

"What?!" He shook his head, protesting, "She's been doing this for the past four months. She requested this hearing and then she doesn't show? Hell no!" He grudgingly took his seat, crossing his legs.

"I don't make the rules, sir. You are not the custodial parent in the case, so you will have to wait."

"Okay, I'll wait," he scoffed, "Again and again. I took off work to be here. Ya'll won't take off the child support because she causes me to lose a day at work. Hell!"

The chatter in the room started to grow again.

"Lori Riggs and Brandon Riggs!" The chatter died down for a second.

"We're here!" someone answered from the wall behind me.

"Okay, you're next." She smiled at them. "Please follow me."

———

A white guy and a black woman filed out behind the short court clerk. They went in, and about ten minutes later, she was the only one walking out.

"Oops! That's another one off to jail for back-child support," someone whispered from behind me.

"Yup, they oughta take care of their children and their baby mommas, then it'd all be okay," someone else answered, "We need money just like those kids do. Shoot."

I wanted to say something on the side of the man, but why should I? I stood in my own case, fighting an uphill battle. Besides, talking to them wouldn't solve a thing. Doors opened, more people walked in; other doors opened, more walked out. Time was passing slowly as I got closer and closer to the edge of frustration.

"Bobby Phillips!" Finally, they called me, "Bobby Phillips!"

"Yes, ma'am?" I got up and walked over to the clerk.

"Sir, is your child's mother, Lisa Gillam, here yet?"

"No, she has not shown up."

"You know that we will have to wait until she appears?"

"I don't think that's correct. I am the custodial parent in this case and I have had my son with me for more than eight months."

"Do you have a lawyer?"

"No, but I have all the documentation that was requested, and now it's time that you guys put her in jail for not showing up this time and the last two times besides."

"Well, let me talk to the judge and see if he would see you without the mother."

I walked back to my seat and sat down beside my boxes. The murmurs were getting louder. When you are in court, you just know that everyone is trying to hear what's going on in someone else's case.

"Excuse me," a woman said as she sat down nest to me, "Do you think it's a good thing for you to pursue your baby's momma like this?"

I wanted to curse her ass out for invading my space.

"First of all, I am not pursuing her. She is not a good mother or parent. She is the mother of our son—not a baby, a son. Secondly, I am doing the same thing that you and all the other women in here are doing—trying to get the best for my child."

"I just think that it's wrong for you to be in court to attack a woman. That's against all the things that God has put in play on this earth."

That's exactly what I thought. This woman is out of her damn mind.

"May I ask who you are and why you are questioning me like this?"

"Oh, sorry. I am Evangelist Veronica Dorrance of the Waymaker Church."

"Well, Ms. Dorrance, was it God's divine prophecy that you be in here with a child I'm guessing was born out of wedlock? Is that your blessing to the world—to overlook your faults and point fingers at other people?"

I hoped my loud tone might shut her up, but no.

"You know the Lord does forgive us of all our sins." She wouldn't shut her mouth.

"Yeah, I do know that, but you are just like your womanizing pastor over at Waymaker Church. Wasn't he convicted of raping one of his members two years ago?"

"I will be praying for you, my brother. You need to be right with the Lord for all your business dealings to work well for you. You're dressed up all nice, but smelling like you got some underhanded things going on. The Spirit is telling me that you have not been dealing with the Lord like you should. You need to repent and get right."

"Girl, why don't you go back in the corner and take care of your own business?"

A small woman shouted from the opposite side of the room, "All you fake-ass church people forget about all the dirt that y'all have done and think that your mess don't stink." She crossed her legs and put a smirk on her face as she added, "You need to pray for yourself and keep your damned legs closed, then you wouldn't be in here with the rest of us. All of us in here begging for pennies from bums that don't care about their children."

Ms. Dorrance got up in silence and walked back over to the corner she came from. There were a few handclaps and enough talking to cause the court clerk to open the door long enough to request silence from the peanut gallery. The room went back to its low roar.

"Just stay out of other people's business," the woman finished.

I looked at her for a minute. I caught her eye and mouthed "Thank you" to her. She smiled, and I put my focus back onto the closed door, trying to mentally push the clerk to come in and call my name so I can get on with my life.

"Cheryl Tank and Brian Waters!" shouted the clerk as the door opened again. She looked at me as her eyes roved around the room. "Cheryl Tank and Brian Waters?" she called out again. "If your party is not here," she called out to no one particular, "Get up and call them, or your cases will be thrown out and you will have to wait at least six months before you can get in to see the judge again."

"Wait!" I called, hurrying to her before she could walk out that door again, "I am here to get full custody of my son. I don't need the other party for that."

"You may be correct. I will ask the judge."

"Thank you."

Planting Daisies

I sat back in the little black chair. A question came to me from the other side of the room and I knew that I had already hit my limit from my encounter with *Sister Save-a-Ho*.

"Hey big boy, why you wanna ruin a sister's life by taking her child and leaving her by herself?"

"Well, it goes this way," I answered. Wanting to make it as plain as I could, I spoke loudly in hopes that not everyone in the room would try to chime into the fray, "I am not trying to leave her by herself. She has done things that have put my son's life in jeopardy and I am not having any of that. I am also not inclined to have to explain myself to someone who doesn't realize that a child is not a paycheck, nor a means to get a good apartment across town. I do understand that the situation you currently find yourself in is by your own design and is the fault of no one but you."

"Wait a minute here!" she tried to cut me off.

"No, you wait a minute. If, let's say, you would have waited until you got married, or at least used some type of protection, you would not be back here again and again and again and again because all your baby daddies are not paying child support, but you are still sleeping with them and expecting them to respect you.

"At some point in time, you have to get some snap about yourself. The time for partying and sleeping with a guy has to be over for two reasons. First, you need to get up off your back and get a job and take of the responsibility that you helped create and get out of my pocket, expecting my tax dollars to keep paying your lights, gas, and water." I looked around the room and realized that I was standing and lecturing, "Second, the next time your baby daddy tries to slide you thirty dollars instead of paying his child support, you need to violate him and send him to jail. Thirty dollars doesn't pay a thing in this world. Good sex and small change, is that all that you're worth?"

"Shawna, you should've kept your mouth shut. He's reading your ass like a TV Guide."

"He ain't nothing. Just because he got on a suit and smells all good. He ain't nothing."

"Yes ma'am," I answered again, "You are correct. I am not nothing. I am somebody who is in love with his son and will raise him to stay away from skanks like you. The days of a brother just falling into any bed has to stop. It is just destroying our whole culture. We are sorry as a group of black people can be. All everybody's trying to do is get something for nothing. You are correct, but you've missed the entire point of our conversation. I grew up in the projects. My mother and father were not married, but they lived together their entire lives. They made me go to college and expected me to do better than they did. I messed up and believed that a girl from the neighborhood could be made to be better. I was wrong, and now my son has to live with the fact that his mother chose drugs over his wellbeing."

"Well, I am sorry for that," Shawna answered smugly, "I didn't know the situation was like that. And I don't give it up for thirty dollars. I ain't no ho."

I ignored her statement.

"If and when you come back in here, come back to take care of your situation. Leave here today with the thought that you should get off the system and make something of yourself instead of re-starting a broken cycle. If you don't understand that, understand this—the things that you do will be done by your children. All the boyfriends that you have, all the sorry good-for-nothing friends that you hang out with, all the times your lights are cut off and you have no water or food in the house—your children will start to see that mess as a normal way of life. Do better. Go to school and better your situation and stop trying to blame everyone else for the dumb decisions you've made."

I took a breath and sat down. Yeah, they talked to each other, but not to me. The murmurings got loud enough that you could hear the judge's gavel strike the bench several times as he shouted at the wall for the participants to all be quiet or be sent home and have their cases reset.

"Bobby Phillips!" The clerk didn't even step fully into the room, "Bobby, could you come with me?"

I nodded and rolled my stack of information behind me. I didn't look back at the room as I left. I didn't owe any of those women a second look. I had had my say and I felt that it should have affected at least one or two in the crowd.

"Have a seat in the front row," she said, pointing to the left side of the room, "The judge will be talking to you next."

I kept an eye on my watch. Ten minutes, then twenty minutes passed. It didn't feel good.

"Mr. Phillips, please come to the counselor's table."

I got up, rolling my four boxes with me. I felt my stomach ball up in knots. I didn't sit.

"Mr. Phillips, the judge is considering placing you in custody for six months for non-payment of child support. Do you have anything you would like to say before you go before the judge?"

"You're damn right I do." I wanted to shout and curse, but I gritted my teeth to explain, "I am not behind on any type of child support. My son lives with me." I looked at the judge. I knew he heard me. "How in the world do you guys screw up like this?"

"Mr. Phillips, approach the bench," beckoned the judge.

"Sir," I said as I walked around the large circular table, "I am not behind in child support. I have all of my receipts and check stubs."

"The paperwork that I am looking at is two years old and it says that you have not made any payments."

"Well, Your Honor, your information is terribly wrong." He looked at the child support attorney and back at me. "Show me what you have, please."

I separated my boxes and placed folder after folder on the table. I handed him a blue folder that contained all my check stubs showing the withdrawals from my pay. He thumbed through the folder, showing no emotion.

"How did this mess happen?" He looked at the clerk and the attorney, then back at me. "What else can you show me that will make me let you walk out of this courtroom, Mr. Phillips?"

I turned and grabbed three folders that showed my son's mother's arrest records, the family court documents that made me the custodial parent, and the hospital records showing the pictures and medical information detailing the twenty stitches my son had to get because of his crack-addict mother.

He took his time. He paused over the police reports and the pictures of my son in the emergency room. His silence cheered me back to calm.

"Mr. Phillips, please have a seat for a moment."

I said nothing. I sat and watched the attorney try to talk his way out of the problem that was now in front of the judge. I heard words like, "This was in another court" and "Are you that incompetent as an attorney?" I wanted to smile, but I just sat and tried to catch every little word so I could get the gist of their conversation.

"Mr. Phillips, please come back."

I stepped up and said nothing. The judge shuffled the folders I had given him.

"Do you know where Ms. Gillam is?"

"I haven't seen her for almost a year."

"How did you file this in her name for increase in support when she is not the custodial parent?" The judge said, turning to glare at the attorney for the AG's office. She just kept shuffling through papers and files. She looked disorganized.

"Your Honor, this was just a mistake in paperwork. My office doesn't always make mistakes like this. I do apologize."

"I will have a talk with your boss. I almost sent a man to jail for something that you screwed up on. Mr. Phillips, I apologize for the error and anger you must feel at this time."

"Your Honor, I just want to get complete custody of my son and close this case for good. Lisa can't do a thing for him. She all but killed him already over a drug deal, and if it weren't for those twenty stitches, he'd be dead now. What else could she offer that would be an asset to my eleven-year-old son?"

"I don't want to take a child away from his mother, but in this case everything points to you being the better parent. My clerk will have your papers ready in ten minutes and the Attorney General's office will not be bothering you after today."

"Thank you, Your Honor."

I sat, relieved of the entire situation. Relieved from knowing that I came close to going to jail, losing my son, losing my job, being put into the system as a deadbeat dad and having a number tagged to my name for the rest of my life. If I didn't love my son so much, I would wish I could take back the night I slept with that girl and put myself in this situation.

Ten minutes turned into fifteen minutes.

"Mr. Phillips," the clerk called me to her little desk, "I had to wait for the judge to sign off on his judgment in your case. I do apologize for the error. We don't get too many dads in here as the custodial parent. You know the assumption is often that all the cases are in favor of the custodial parent, no matter what the non-custodial parent has done to make things better."

"I can see that now." She stamped the papers and smiled at me.

"I am really sorry that we held you up for so long for something that should have been handled in twenty minutes. We did make the mistake. It's just that you were being scheduled to be taken into custody. That's why we had you wait so long," she explained, smiling again, "I am sorry for any problems this might have caused you."

In my mind I was cursing and telling her to shut the hell up.

"I'm okay." I smiled. "I do thank you for apologizing and getting the paperwork done so quickly. By the way, will the support stop coming out of my check?"

"Yes, it will. I faxed all the correct documentation to your employer, just as the judge ordered. The Child Support Offices will file paperwork to have Ms. Gillam repay the support she has received for the last year."

I gathered the papers from her, strapped my boxes to my little dolly, and strolled out. Lisa was a crack addict. Repayment was not a word in her vocabulary. As soon as I got to my car, I called my son. He couldn't wait to hear all the happenings of the day, and we screamed excitedly into each other's ear. I promised him that I would never let failure come between us. I owed him that much. I left him with a woman that had a serious problem with taking care of responsibilities. We made plans for the weekend. We got off the phone with him telling me that he had to go work on a paper because he wanted to be done by the time I got home.

Home. "Home" is a word that we take for granted. My son is at home. "Oh, to play the blues and not be sad," that's what my dad used to say when he'd sit on the porch with his Red Stripe beer and record player, just looking back at the things he had gotten over.

The Cycle of Life

There she goes again.

Sitting in the corner of the couch so she can watch him bumble and stumble around in the kitchen.

She sits there in silence.

She lets the tears fall from her face to the soft material of the couch.

She does not move a muscle or make any sudden movements.

He might see her.

He might just come after her again.

Beat on her.

Call her names.

Spit on her.

Rape her.

Tell her that she is not worth a damn.

But this is the woman he told everyone in the church he would cherish, adore, and take care of for the rest of her life.

She looks at him in the kitchen, eating his food and grumbling at the way it has been prepared. She wants to shout at him. She wants to call him a pig. She wants to put on her shoes and run home. But the last time she ran home, her dad called him to come get her and fix his problem. He was told to train her to be the wife she is supposed to be.

She now realizes that the man in the kitchen is the copy of the man that raised her and beat her mother to death. She wants to scream for help. She cannot. She cannot find her own strength any more. She used to be so strong and beautiful. She thinks about all the debate club trophies she once had. She thinks about all the track meets she ran in. She thinks about the guy she did not want because he did not want to party and drink. That guy never asked her out a second time.

She jumps as she hears the dishes hit the sink and break. He tells her he is going to take a bath and that the kitchen better be cleaned before he gets out of the tub. She waits to move. She waits to hear the water spill out on the floor. Then she makes her move. She sweeps. She washes. She dries. She prepares his lunch for the next day. She sits back in the corner of the couch and listens to him sing. She wishes he would drown. She looks out the window and cries. Her tears are broken when she hears the floor creak. Her heart stops when she sees her three-year-old daughter has wet herself again.

She sees her daughter living the life she is now in. The light bulb comes on. She makes her move. She grabs the bag that has been packed in the closet for three months. She changes her daughter. She wipes tear tracks from her face. She offers him a beer while he is in the tub. He accepts. She makes the exchange in silence and locks the bathroom door as she leaves.

There is a "Sshhhhh baby," and "Do you want to go for a ride?"
She grabs the bag and the baby and turns the television on.
She opens the back door.
She leaves out the front door.
She makes it to the corner just as the bus is pulling up.
She does not look back.
They sing together.
They sing "The Wheels on the Bus."

6
A Spoon and a Flashlight

THERE WERE TWO BUDDIES WHO WENT OUT FISHING, AS THEY USU-
ally did. By the end of their early morning, they were tired, but happy with the haul that they had gotten. They started on their return
through the woods to their truck. Fishing in the early morning sun
can be tiring. They walked and talked. Busy with their conversation,
they missed the tree that held the small red triangles that marked
the place that they should have turned left instead of right.

After a few minutes of walking, the two realized the woods
around them were unfamiliar. The two decided to follow the sun
and continued on. A few minutes passed by, and then the two van-
ished from the view of the sun, birds, and the clouds that covered
their trail in shade.

Several hours had passed. Waking in pain, one friend turned
to the other and asked, "Brad, what in the world happened?"

"I can't tell you a thing," Brad moaned, "I truly don't remember
falling into this hole. I think my ankle may be broken." Fumbling
for his small keychain flashlight, Brad asked, "How are we gonna
get out of here?"

"It looks like we're stuck at the beginning of a well of some
type here," his friend answered as the light shone against the walls.
The man looked around several times, wishing something would

change. "I don't see a way out of here. I don't think we can climb out, the opening is just too high."

"Cliff, I don't think we can scream loud enough to attract any help. We are way off the trail.

Silence overtook the two men.

"Brad!" Cliff shouted in excitement, "I got a spoon! I got a spoon!"

Brad turned his back and laid still. His only movements were the skittering of the little flashlight hitting the mud wall.

"Go on and play with your spoon," Brad groaned, playing with the flashlight all the while, "we'll be dead in a few days anyway."

Time went by. The only sound that could be heard over the moaning and groaning was a low, constant scratching.

Scratch! Scratch! Scratch!

"Why don't you just sit still rather than play with your spoon? It's becoming annoying, you know?"

No words came from Cliff. The only sounds he produced were the scratching noises of his spoon throughout the long night. No words were exchanged between the two friends.

The sun peeked down into the pit. Brad woke and looked for Cliff, surprised to see no sign of him at the bottom of the pit. He immediately tried to jump to his feet, remembering too late that both feet were swollen. He sat back down. He thought to himself that his anger at Cliff almost masked his the pain that should have overwhelmed his being so selfish. As he looked up, he saw a glimpse of Cliff's legs leaving the top of the pit.

"Cliff! Cliff!"

No answer came from his friend, only a brief appearance of Cliff's head followed by more silence. After what seemed like hours and numerous screams of frustration, Brad found himself curled back into his little ball, still playing with his little flashlight. He dozed off and woke up several times to watch the sun's progress across the sky through the top of the pit.

"He left me to die."

The brightness of the sky came and went. Tears flowed into open cries. Those cries went into prayers begging for forgiveness of long-forgotten sins and faults. Then silence wrapped its arms around Brad. He slept, and cried in his sleep. He accepted the fate of death. He and his little flashlight continued their play until its battery went to sleep too.

Thwap!

The pain of something falling onto his back made him sit up in terror. He looked up and saw several black-looking figures peering down at him from the top of the pit.

"Hey are you through crying for the night?" Brad didn't care who it was talking to him.

He was just happy to hear someone's voice.

"Who is it?"

"Well, it's not the Lord, if that's who you're looking for?"

"What is this you dropped on me?"

"It's a harness. Put it on and make sure you fasten all the straps tightly. We need to get you out of that hole before it starts raining any harder," the voice called down.

"Okay." He put his keys in his pocket and put the harness on as quickly as he possibly could. "Where is Cliff? Is Cliff with you?"

"No. Cliff is not with us," the voice yelled back, "Do you have the straps on?"

"Yes. Yes, I do!" Brad sat up straight and waited for more instructions. "What happened to my friend Cliff? Did he send you to me?"

"Take hold of the rope and hold on." The rope immediately tightened. "Do not let go of the rope. It's just in case you didn't tighten all the straps on the harness, okay?"

"Okay!"

There was a jerk and then a slow and steady rise to the top. Brad was happy to be rescued, but the thought of how he had treated his friend in the past and the things he had said and thought of him since he'd left made him feel like dirt. Reaching the top, he felt several hands grab on the straps and his arms to end his nightmare in the pit.

"Sir, are you okay? Do you need to call anybody before we take you to the hospital?"

"Yeah." He looked around and noticed that there were no men in the rescue party.

"Where is my friend? Is he okay?"

"Your friend is in the hospital. He's safe." They unstrapped him, helped him into the back of a four-wheeler, and headed off. "You are a lucky man."

"Yeah, I know," Brad answered as he looked up to the heavens to say thank you, "God is a good God."

"No, not that," the woman continued, "Your friend had two broken legs, and somehow he climbed out of that hole and made it the three miles to flag down my car. If he would have stopped, he would have died before alerting anyone. I don't think anyone ever comes to these back trails anymore."

"I don't know what to say." His stomach was in knots.

"He did tell us how much he loves your friendship and that after this is all over, he would start going to church with you and your family."

"How can he think about church? I cursed him and called him all kinds of names. How can he still want to be my friend? I turned my back on him. I didn't listen to him at all."

The women put Brad into the back of a car and buckled him in. Sleep was heavy on his eyes. He couldn't fight it off. They asked for his home phone number several times. He remembered murmuring something, but not clearly.

"Sir, this is Paris and Doobie. They will take you to the hospital."

Brad took a deep breath and went to sleep.

"Brad?" He opened his eyes to see a familiar face. "Are you feeling okay? They said that you won't be able to dance anymore."

"Shoot, I don't care. I can't dance anyhow."

The friends laughed as they discussed their ordeal and the neat stitches that were a welcome sight. Their friendship grew and was better for it.

Moral of the Story

No matter how small your light, it can always help someone else, even in the midst of your own storms.

7

The Rider

"MARLIN, MARTEL, PATIENCE! COME IN THE KITCHEN! I NEED YOU guys right now!"

"Yeah, Mom? What's wrong?"

"Just sit and listen. I just found this recording your father left for us."

Click!

"Sandra, I know that this is hard for you to listen to. By this time, I should have been gone for a week or so. I am recording this while you guys are in the pool and having a good time. This is not the way thing were supposed to be. I sit and watch my kids play in the backyard while my body is decaying by the day. Stuck in this stupid wheelchair, limited—limited in life and love. I hate this thing, but it's the only way I can move about the house."

Ring! Ring!

"I have already resolved in my mind that I will not be answering any calls while you and the kids are outside. I want to see them playing as much as I can. I have always liked to see you smile in the sun. You are still as good-looking as the day we met. Not as fine, but good-looking anyhow. I think three kids have worn out that frame, or maybe it was me—"

"Hey Dad! Watch this dive!"

"That's Martel shouting at me, if you couldn't recognize his voice . . . "

"Be careful!"

" . . . It was really an ugly dive into the pool. All I can do is smile and nod. I hate the hell out of Lou Gehrig and his disease. I have no way to fight out of this living tomb. That's why I am leaving you this, along with the envelope it's taped to—"

"Dad, this dive's gonna be better! Watch this!"

"I'm trying to keep the recorder out of sight. I don't want you walking in here and checking on me because you see something in my hand. I have been moving my hand just a little each of the past few days. I wanted enough strength and practice so I could let you hear how I am feeling and how much I truly love you. I do hope that you will replay this for the kids to hear later on.

"Now to business, my time is limited with this good hand. In the envelope you will find the insurance policy I told you about two years ago. Two years ago—when I was still able to walk, go to work, and not be the burden I have become to you. "

"Stan, you were never a burden to me," Sandra murmured, drawing the kids closer as they listened.

"Don't say a word, just listen. The insurance policy has an accidental death and dismemberment clause attached to it. Sandra, wait to read it. I am still talking to you. I know how you like to try and see and think that you are hearing what I am saying."

"Okay, okay," Sandra sighed, "It's like you are still watching me . . ."

"The rider only pays in the result of an accident. I died from the disease taking my life away. We both know that I would have ended up a total vegetable in the end. This is why it had to be this way. Don't get upset, just keep listening. You guys can never tell anyone what I've done. I made this choice because the bills were too high from the doctor visits and the fights with the insurance company were taking a toll on my sanity.

"Two years ago, I thought that we would pray upon a miracle, but the miracle is in the envelope in your mother's hands. The policy pays four hundred and six thousand dollars. I had taken the extra coverage at work and paid it up for four years from my 401K.

I thought this was a good investment in my family's future. I wanted you guys to be able to go to college and not worry about the burden of paying the bills alone. Now, if you guys would just get some scholarships, it would mean more cash for you once you graduate.

"Now, you and I both know they're not going to be in sports! You guys got the under-achiever sports genes from your mom's side of the family. Just look at your Aunt Raniesha and your Uncle Sam. Remember how they tried to play softball at the last family reunion?"

"He is right about that!"

"Yeah, Mom couldn't run to base to save her life!"

"Hush, Marlin and Martel, we want to hear this through."

"What has happened should never be found out, because they should have come and taken the chair and repaired the broken and burned wires in the motor. They wont ask any questions since the chair was a rental and had been used several times before me. Yes, I did rig the chair to short out. I only hope that it happened in the house and not in the street. I would have hated to have been run over by a car or something. I wanted to go out intact, with my unmovable back or neck broken beyond repair.

"We did agree to no machine keeping this body of mine alive and my mind not functioning in any capacity."

Ring! Ring! Ring!

"That daggum phone will not stop. I don't have much time. I think you heard it, but you're still out at the pool with that puzzled look on your face. You look at me. So I am showing you all my teeth to keep you sitting there while I finish here."

Ring! Ring!

"There will not be a message. I will delete whoever called and left one. This is too important and I don't want anything to deter me. I rewired the motor two weeks ago. You remember the day that you found me under the bed and ask how I fell?"

"Yes, I do. Damn, something told me to look under the bed and I didn't."

"Listen, it's not your fault—I had to distract you. It hurt like hell to get down to the floor, but my plan had been in place for longer than you can realize. Sandra, I want the best for you. That doesn't mean I want you to go out and get a replacement anytime soon! I will sit on the edge of the bed and haunt you. I really can't see you having someone else love you besides me . . . "

"Oh, that is way too much information."

"You kids know how y'all got here. Don't think it's disgusting that your parents had to do the huck-a-buck to get you guys here."

"My brain is on fire!"

"I didn't want to ever think about that!"

"Haaaaa! It's like Dad is still here being silly."

"I know how you guys feel, but listen!"

" . . . I want this to be a smooth transition so you guys can live better now than when I was around this last year. All the times y'all wouldn't shut up and talk to me about things that I didn't really want to hear was both an agony and a pleasure. Patience, leave the dumb boys alone and focus on your eleventh-grade year. You are too smart to deal with a fool at this stage of your life. Find someone who has you and your dreams in mind. Martel and Marlin, don't make any babies! You have one year left in high school. Do the best for me and your mother. You guys make sure your mother is happy—alone, but happy. We don't need an Uncle Seymour in the house until you guys are in college.

"The check should be in the mail by the time you are listening to me say these goodbyes. This is not the way I wanted to go. I wanted to be at least ninety and have twelve or thirteen grandchildren, with you kids happily married as I have been with your mother.

"I want to thank you guys for being the best family around. You were better than the clowns that I grew up with. I love you more than words can tell. Since this is the end of my mission, I'll admit how glad I am that you can only hear me and not see how badly this good arm is beginning to shake. I want to tell you guys that I truly love you and will love you through eternity. I didn't leave letters anywhere else in the house—you have to check the safe-deposit box at the credit union. They have been there for a year. Do not open them until Christmas."

"Christmas? That's months away!"

"I have to go. I see you guys are wrapping things up at the pool, but remember I will always be in your memories and heart through the love we have for each other. I told no one else of this, and neither should you. People speak way too much of other folks' business, and you guys know how I hate rumors and gossip."

"Yeah, we know . . . "

"Patience, hush!"

"Okay, okay!"

"There will be no other record of how the chair was broken. So if the insurance company calls, don't say a word to them. I have prayed and prayed on what I should do. I couldn't wait any longer for an answer. It was my decision. Forgiveness is of the Lord. I just hope that I can be at the great feast in the end. If not, I did my best for you guys, and I hope that the money replaces what I am unable to provide for you.

"Please take care of one another. Respect one another. Boys, do not let any man put his hands on your sister. Honey, I love you. Gotta go now, bye."

"*BEEEEEEEEEEEEEEEEEEEEEEEP!*"

"Is it over. There isn't any more?"

"Wait, I hear rustling."

"Uh, *BEEEEEEEEEEEEEEEEEEEEEEEEEEEP!*"

"That's dad making that noise!"

"He always knew how to get a laugh out of a bad situation."

"Bye, guys. I just wanted to put a smile on your face before I shut this thing off."

Click . . .

8
Considered Me?

Knock, knock, knock!

I found myself at her door, upset and confused at the news. I knew it was late, but there was no one on the road by Elisa's house.

Knock, knock, knock! I knew I was hitting the door too hard. I should have the right.

"*Elisa!*" I screamed in my mind before it came out my mouth, "Please open the door!"

A light came on and lit up the front window. The chain rattled as it fell from its fasteners. The click from the dead bolt as the doorknob unlocked overwhelmed my anger. As she opened the door, I noticed that she still had her uniform on. The hospital logo was a brilliant, eye-catching blue. I could see the trails of tears that broke the makeup that made her face look smooth. My heart dropped. All the time I had known her, she had always been a natural beauty.

"Can I come in and talk to you?"

The silence was only shattered by the squeak of the door's hinges. She stepped back and gestured for me to take a seat on the couch.

"Do you want something to drink?" she asked as she started toward the kitchen, "'Cause I sure need something."

"Sure." A drink would give me time to get my words together.

"Water or juice?" she yelled from the next room.

"Juice, thank you!"

She came back, handed me a Styrofoam cup, and sat down on the couch.

"What do you want to talk about?"

"I have heard some things from your mother . . . But I don't believe that I can persuade you to change your mind in the least bit, can I?"

"No, not really." Her pause was deafening. "It doesn't have anything to do with you."

"I beg to differ." I drank from the cup: one sip to clear my throat and another two to keep myself from cussing before saying carefully, "It took the both of us to get to this point in this situation, so why wouldn't I matter?"

"It was a mistake that can't be corrected."

"You're right, but not totally. It's the two of us that are in this and it should be a decision between the both of us before you talk to other people."

"Boy, don't kid yourself. You don't love me, and I am not in love with you." She took a drink from her soda. "All this boils down to is that we hung out for two days and had sex. There's nothing more than that in this situation for the two of us to talk about. You can't add any emotional ties to what we've done. It was just sex."

"I think you should have called me the first time it crossed your mind. You've called on me to fix your flats and other stuff before we did the deed. If you didn't want me, you should have called other folks and talked to them about that, right? I do believe we could become a serious couple if we work at it. I think—"

"—No, you hold on!" She stopped and took a drink from her soda again before going on, "You're not thinking. I am not doing the nine-month thing to have you change your mind about your responsibilities and leave me alone to raise a child."

"I'm not like that. You know me." I moved to touch her hand. She jerked it away from my reach. "I want to do the right thing. No matter how hard I have to work. Look how long we have been down for each other." I took a breath and tried to calm down—I couldn't. "Damn!"

"The right thing is for me to leave you alone, usher you out my house and life, and hit the reset button. I still have time to correct this mess." She put the can on the table before continuing, "I am not ready for a child to be in my life. I want to be free to do whatever the hell I want to do and not be locked down to some man or a snotty-nosed brat. Look at this world: women are being conned into being stuck with children that they can't handle and got because the brother didn't want to use protection. I don't want to be in any position where you leave me alone and without paying child support on the regular. We're not married. You are not committed to me, and I am not having a baby right now."

"Girl, you are systematically stupid!" I took a breath and lowered my tone. The look on her face was boldly uncaring. "Let me say this, there is this belief that all men are in the self-same boat of making babies and leaving them behind. There are a great many of us who were raised to believe that a woman is a gift from God." She sat back on the couch in silence as I said my piece, "Yes, we had sex, and the result is that we find ourselves in this discussion. Our choices have faced us with a range of problems, but this is the hand that we have been dealt. This isn't a simple decision for you to make or handle alone. I am here."

"I do understand how you feel."

"No, you don't." I felt mad. "No, you do not. You don't understand that a child, in or out of wedlock, is more than the chance to receive a monthly stipend. It's a life to be nurtured and cherished. There has been this destruction of the role of the man in his child's life. Look at the popular television shows in this country. The man is either gone from the home or he is an idiot who can't put a simple sandwich together without burning down the kitchen. I am more than that. Did you at least consider my feelings?" I was trying to keep my tone low and consistent. It wasn't working, "You do realize there's a system in place that's making the black man extinct in this nation? If he is not hooked on drugs or alcohol, he is locked up for five to ten years—whether he did the crime or not.

"The idea of being institutionalized demoralizes anyone after a time. It destroys the self-esteem and self-efficacy to the point that these men just give up. It's hard to get ahead when you know that when people look at you wearing a suit on the street, they either think you are a preacher or on your way to or from court. The male population of our culture is being rendered useless, and as a result, we are not considered responsible enough to take care of a family. Did you consider me in this? That's my question to you. Did you, even in the smallest corner of your mind?"

She sat for a long while before she said anything.

"I am not my father!" She said nothing in response. "I am nothing like my father." I gripped the Styrofoam cup. I wanted to squeeze its contents to the floor. I took a deep breath, "Say something!"

She wasted no time answering.

"You are gonna have to leave." She stood and walked toward the door. "It's late and I have to go to work in the morning. I don't know what else to tell you right now."

As I walked through the door, I asked again, "Did you consider me outside of all those other people's wrongs that you think could come from being with me?"

"No, I didn't consider you before I had them kill our son two days ago."

She slammed the door and locked it.

It took an hour for me to make the fifteen-minute drive to my apartment.

9

Paper versus Plastic

IF WE WOULD LEARN TO SIT AND THINK ABOUT LIFE THE WAY OTH-
ers think about first loves, a new car, or starting a new career, the art
of looking for failure in others would not come as easily as second
nature.

I sat down and listened to the whir of the computer's fan over
the sound of the slowly uploading pictures of my family. I liked
having updated shots about every six months or so. To look at our
growth over the past twelve years is amazing. Pictures are one way
I know we can leave memories our children will be able to pass on
long after we are gone. It is something Sherman and I talked about
after we had Price, our eldest son.

Looking at the small box of old mail Sherman has been keeping for months and months, I decided to go through it and put
them into some type of order for him—and ease my curiosity over
why most of them hadn't been opened yet. The pictures could wait.

The first of them were cards I had given him over the past two
years . . . I was surprised he kept them. Several at the bottom were
from his Dad. They were more than five years old. From before he
passed. All were opened. I couldn't bring myself to read them. The
bulk of the mail was from Myoma State Bank, all unopened. I knew
we didn't have an account there, so I sorted them by date. They went

back almost six years. Six years, and he hadn't said anything to me about having a separate account.

"Okay, okay," I told myself, "It's not like he's been stashing cash to leave."

I took a few deep breaths as all kinds of thoughts made my nerves boil. I took out several rubber bands and bound the different stacks of envelopes together before placing them back into the box. Surely he would see this and tell me what the letters from the bank meant. Why the secrets in the first place? I felt like calling Cassandra and asking her advice, but this wasn't public business. So I didn't.

I left it alone. I went back to printing out the pictures and placed them in the little four-by-five-inch frames I'd picked up from the Family Dollar. We had a dedicated wall in the den for family photos. After all these years, it was becoming a bit of a chore to rearrange the wall. But I loved doing it.

Two days came and went before Sherman thanked me for organizing "my box," as he called it. He offered no explanation of the contents. We'd eaten three dinners together, and still no word about that box. I didn't know what's boiling in me more, anger or curiosity. I thought I'd give it a month before I brought up the issue to him.

I was out in the back sorting laundry. That's my Saturday morning thing to do. Sherman washes the cars, cuts that grass, and plays with the kids. That's all after they've had their fill of the Cartoon Network.

Thumbing through the mail, I found another letter from the bank. I held it up so I could see some of the wording. Maybe I could piece together some of the contents. It took me a minute. I was trying to look through the white envelope and watch for anyone coming trough the door.

"Shoot!" It was too thick to read through. I put the small pile of mail down and took the Cato catalog to the washroom with me.

"I know what that mess is!" I said to myself as I dropped the catalog into the towel basket, "That's got to be posted checks!"

I knew I shouldn't open it, but we were married. There shouldn't be any secrets.

I walked back into the laundry room to sit down and placed the letter on the little table I set up for my hideaway. I stared at the print for what seemed to be ten minutes. I opened it; I didn't care if I tore the envelope. I wasn't hiding what I'd decided to do.

In between the pounding of my heart and trying not to be nervous, I thumbed through copies of checks and a six-page bank statement. I felt beads of sweat run down my face.

"*Nerves,*" I told myself, "behave yourselves. Sherman's not telling me something we all should know." I *should* know. The question I didn't want to answer kept knocking at the door of my intuition. I didn't want to acknowledge her at all.

"I don't think he's got another life going," I whispered as I continued to scan the large-font copies, "He just doesn't seem the type. He's here most of the time." I tried to stay above the rising flood of anger that was slowly seeping up over my thoughts and rationality. As I went about my wifely chores, my thoughts kept getting swept toward the negative.

So many thoughts about how to confront the situation.

So many different ways to pack and leave.

So many ways to read his ass bare.

So many ways to destroy our family by telling our kids that their Dad doesn't want to be with us anymore.

After all this self-persuasion, I got up the nerve to call Sherman in from outside. He came without any hesitation. The children followed. I said nothing. I walked to the kitchen, poured some juice, and made them a snack before retreating to my hideaway to wait for Sherman, letter in hand.

He came in still smiling from playing with the children. I struggled for words for a few minutes, not sure how to start. My heart and thoughts went from anger to sadness to loneliness. I handed him the opened envelope and waited for some kind of response. Several deep breathes and several more minutes crawled by in silence before I could get any words out. I couldn't wait anymore.

"I don't believe that you could be so high-and-mighty that you refuse to open your mouth about this bank account. Isn't this marriage supposed to be based upon trust and communication?" He said nothing. "I'm ready to walk out. You've not so much as given me a single sign that you're worried about us continuing on as a family—I should just take the children and go without another word."

He opened the statement. Read it. Put it back into the envelope. Folded it and stuck it in his back pocket.

"You've nothing to say about this? I'm getting even more pissed by your silence and the way you're looking at me. I am really beginning to believe all those things my sister said to look for over all these years. How long have you been cheating on me? How long have you been living a lie?"

Now that I'd started, I couldn't stop myself, "How in the world could you do this to me? What in the world have I done to you that I—no, me and our *children*—should deserve to be treated like used socks?"

BZZZZZ! The dryer broke my tirade.

"If this is your decision," he said in that controlled way of his, "do you want me to get the big suitcase out for you?"

His words threw me.

"If this is how you come to see me, through the eyes of your sister's warped sense of how a relationship should be, I'll go and make sure the van is full of gas and tuned up before you leave. I am okay with whatever you decide. What do you want me to do?"

I couldn't say a word. I couldn't think beyond the emotions eruptions erupting inside me.

"If you can take the advice of a sister who has never been married, has shacked up with more men than Samson killed with a donkey's jawbone, moved I-don't-know-how-many times, and hasn't been in this house in more than five years—but still has the audacity to tell you how we should be with each other—then I don't know what to say to you.

"And to top all of that mess off, you don't talk to me about a box of letters and receipts that has been on that dresser for half a decade? I am confused. You think I am cheating based on what? Your sister's pompous dreams of us failing? I think you should start following her advice and spend your time following me, snooping around your own house, and then report back to her what you think you may have found. Do you think for one moment that would enhance our relationship? When have I ever not let you know any-thing and everything that was important to our household and the way we live?"

I could not say a word. I looked at his hands and got my nerves back in line. His answers and questions had cut me deep. Sixteen years we'd been working on always leaving space for our own identities, and he'd never questioned me when I went out with my girlfriends or my sisters. He only asked that I call before I pulled into the drive so he could watch me come into the house. That was after a few women in our town were beaten and robbed after being followed home.

"Sherman, why can't I know about the account and the Happy Times Hotel?"

He chuckled.

"Happy Times is not a hotel." He opened the envelope and pulled out the copy of the bank statement, shaking his head. "Happy Times is a hospice."

"A hospice? For who? For what?"

"This is something I had promised my dad and mom would never come out. No one in the family knows anything about this."

"Why?" I looked at his face and I could see the hurt coloring his skin tone.

"It goes like this," he started, taking a breath without raising his head to look at me, "My parents had a child that is older than Kirby. She is severely handicapped and has to have round-the-clock care. That's why the bank account exists. That's why there is a box of receipts and bank statements. That's why I would take my dad out every week for those six months before he went home. And that's why I have never raised this conversation with you. It was a promise between my parents and me. She is the reason why I cut the grass so early on Saturday mornings. It allows me to talk to a sister I've only known for a short while."

I felt like a boob.

"How could you not trust me enough to keep this away from me?"

"Okay, case in point," he answered, looking me in the eye, "Remember some time ago when I was called out to work at three in the morning, and in my rush get to work, I zipped my woody?"

"Yeah, I do." I smiled because he had cried like a girl. "And so?"

"And so? How long was it before you told not only your sisters, but both sides of the family? Everyone knew not two days after it happened."

"Okay, you have got to let it go! It was funny and needed to be shared."

"Funny, but very personal."

"Okay, you think those two things compare?" I was trying to get back to the subject.

"Not the events. It is a known fact that you can't hold water. Remember when we opened the getaway account? How long was it before you told your sister how much we had socked away and where we planned to go?"

I shrugged my shoulders. He had me.

"Six months."

"Alright! So why not just tell everyone about your sister? Your parents have been gone for ten and six years. You have kept your promise."

"Oda is not really up to a lot of people. It took more than seven months for her to look my way when I started taking Dad there."

"Her name is Oda?"

"Actually, it's Rhoda. She has a problem with the letter 'r.' So I just call her Oda. It makes her smile."

Silence came suddenly. Both machines stopped at the same time. The buzzers' shouts were overwhelming.

"Look, next time you want to confront me about anything, talk to me before you deduce the wrong answers to your questions. You almost lost *us*." He stood still for a second and turned for the door. "I know this coming from when you finally went through the box. The only thing that has impressed me is that you only opened one envelope and didn't rush off to the hospice on your own. If I were to cheat on us, she would have to be one hell of a woman to be better than you in anything. I would never want to lose you or us over twenty minutes of sweaty pleasure." He stared into my eyes before telling me, "I love you more than you could ever think."

He walked out, closing the door behind him. I took a breath and started thinking on how to incorporate his sister into our lives and us into hers. If she can handle more visitors, I want her and the children to connect and know one another. I'm gonna talk to Sherman about this again. This is just the beginning of our change, and our promise.

Click!

"Sherman!" His hand snaked back from the light switch as he ran off. "You are not funny!"

10

Cryptic Events

THE SKY STILL LOOKS THE SAME. EACH AND EVERY TIME WE GET out to meet the new arrivals. I like the scenery. It is nice and calming at sunset. No matter how many times I have seen it, it is always beautiful.

"Hurry up, Clyde!" I said, "The sun is setting and you're missing it! And then there are new members arriving tonight."

"Naomi, there's no rush. They'll be here as long as we will be here." He was always grumpy when he first starts to separate and move. "There is no exit from this place, and I have looked at the same sunset for the past ten years. It is becoming redundant. The only thing that changes is the number of birds on the telephone lines."

We started our little walk over to the forum. We never walked fast. It's always the same pace: slow and methodical.

"Don't be such a dweeb." The door opened and belted out a squeak that could shatter the eardrum. "We need some type of excitement while we are still here, waiting."

We walked a little quicker than usual. I guess it seemed almost new because it had been so long since we had to welcome anyone.

"Okay, let's sit in the third row this time." She smiled at me. "We can get a real close look at the NADs this time."

Her eyes seemed to jump like a two-year-old at the circus for the first time. Amazement was in everything she looked at. I almost dove into the waters of her enjoyment. But pity kept me from seeing the joy of welcoming people to this dungeon-like life.

"Wait, there are two seats in the front row!" She was skipping as she said, "I knew there was a reason I liked you, Clyde." She grabbed my hand. "Hurry. Sit! Sit, Sit! It's starting!"

Blam! Blam! Blam! The shaft of the sergeant at arms seemed to shout as it hit the floor of Citizen's empty marble tomb.

"Okay, you nosey people—it's time to welcome the lord of the manor. He's the one that's been here longer than anyone else, the head cheese . . . Dr. Duane Rollins!"

He stepped out of the way. Out came Rollins. I only call him Rollins, because we got here at the same time. We were all in the same boat that sank in the Gulf. Rollins took his place on the makeshift stage and nodded. The shouts for the newly arrived dead grew louder and louder.

"*NADs! NADs! NADs!*"

I have become bored with this type of thing all over again. "Naomi, I really want to leave," I whispered. She paid me no mind, except to roll her eyes as she shouted with the crowd.

"*NADs! NADs! NADs!*"

Blam! Blam! Blam! The staff had spoken again.

"Okay, okay!" Rollins was taking charge, "Bring in the Newly Arrived Dead!"

The hush that came slapped everyone's lips with silence. In walked four lively-looking characters. *NADs* are funny because they still don't realize that this is the final step for some time. But that depends on what you believe and who might just call you back. The shouting came again as they took their places.

"*NADs! NADs!*"

They were led in by the last group of *NADs*. We don't get a lot of new ones, so we kinda recycle the laughter. This cemetery is three hundred years old and overgrown in a lot of places. No one cares about you when you're dead and gone.

"We want to welcome our new guests to the community of the faithfully departed." Rollins pointed at the first person in line and then to the microphone. "Please, everyone, let's listen to how our first guest came to take up residence with us."

The crowd and Naomi finally shut the hell up.

"Hi y'all, I'm Jackson, and I'm an alcoholic."

"Hahahaaa!" The crowd, including myself, burst into sarcastic laughter. His wet appearance was explanation enough to make us keep laughing. "Need a drink?" came a shout from the back of the room.

He cleared his throat and continued, "My name is Jackson, and I've been sober for one day: today. Yesterday I fell off the wagon and took a drink." He paused for a minute. He caught sight of his feet. I am guessing the no shoes thing took the focus from him.

"I knocked back some drinks, not really thinking that my two-and-a-half years of sobriety would have made me blackout so badly. I was just feeling low and thought that if I could just get drunk for a minute, the pain would ease up. Just one more time would end the pangs in my head for just a little while.

"Just a break," he paused for a second as he took in his sur-roundings, "Just a break, just for a minute, just to think on all the things that I lost by falling into the bottle the first time."

He was definitely off. There was no sorrow in this place. We had all made dumb-ass choices when we were alive. Some of us lived full lives, but the majority of us chose to get here early.

"Well," he continued, "I guess with a little more time and help from all of you, I will be able to get back on that horse—get my family and job and stuff back."

The laughter started all over again. He stepped back into the line of four. He smiled, waved, and pointed at people as if he were seeking votes in a political race. With a point from Rollins, the next person stepped to the mic.

"Hi, I am Powers!" he shouted above the laughter.

"Hi, Powers!" The back of the room let him have it. Their an-swers were filled with snickers and laughs.

"I don't know why I am in an AA meeting, or how I got here." The laughter started all over again as he went on, "I only remember that I was in a car accident and passed out when I heard the sirens.

I do admit that I did have those two drinks with dinner . . . But that shouldn't be the reason why I ended up here."

"Is that all?" someone yelled from the back of the room, "Who were you with when you had those two little drinks?"

He smiled before he spoke, as if he were trying to relive the moment.

"I was out with the fellas when I realized I needed to be back at the house. It was getting too late for me to be out."

"Hold up, you jerk!" a woman called out from the back of the group, "I was with you in the car when you wrecked. You lying bastard. You told me that you weren't married. You told me that you didn't like children—and you had four! You lying, good-for-nothing, two-minute ride!"

"Sharon?!" He did look shocked. "Why are you in an AA meeting?"

"AA? You killed us trying to get home to you fat-ass wife. I've been here for six years waiting for them to unplug your machine." His face went pale as she went on, "Seven months. Seven months you played with my emotions. I should've followed my first instincts and said no when you asked me out. I wish I would have followed my intuition that you were bad news . . ."

"Aw, shut up Sharon!" a woman from the back row screamed, "If most of us would have thought before we acted, we wouldn't be stuck down here either. There are no tears left, so shut up and make the best of the time we all have to spend together."

Applause went up and died out. Powers walked back to his place in line and dropped his head. Jackson looked like someone had just burst his favorite red balloon. No one said a word for a second.

Blam! Blam! The four in line shuddered as the sergeant at arms's staff shouted once more.

A young woman walked to the mic. She gave a small nervous smile to us and began to speak, "Hi, I am Tanecia, and I know that I am dead."

"Boo! Boo!" came the collective jeer.

"You are a waste of skin!" I yelled that one. I hate self-takers. They don't consider the people they leave behind. I say it because my girlfriend decided to kill the both of us and not clue me in to the decision. I haven't talked to her for six years now. Her excuse was that it was just "too much pressure going to school, working, and having to sustain a meaningful relationship all at the same time." Bull crap!

"I didn't think it would get to this." The booing continued as she spoke "I am—well, I was—a nice person. I couldn't talk to my parents or my teachers. They wouldn't have understood that I didn't feel accepted by anyone at school." The booing didn't stop. "They didn't like me because I was too skinny, my hair was too frizzy, and I didn't have the right clothes to fit in."

She started crying. Down here it's a waste. We have no tears. We have no fluids in our system. We are just here.

"You didn't fit in?!" The boo's only got louder in response to her crying. "The problem was that you didn't think. It was a selfish act that you can't take back. Get back in line!"

"Wait!" she yelled back, "I tried to kill myself five times before, and no one ever took the time to tell me what to do." That statement didn't help. "They took me to shrinks and gave me antidepressants, but I wasn't having that. I wanted them to tell me how I could be like everybody else. I wanted to fit in."

"Well, from today on, you are exactly like everyone else down here," Rollins spoke, "You got results on your sixth attempt. You are dead."

Applause rose and died after a minute or so. I joined in the laughter. Stupid, just stupid . . .

Blam! Blam! The staff of the sergeant at arms always kills the mood.

Rollins motioned to the next person in line to step to the mic. She did. She moved slowly, scratching and shaking the entire time. Her hair looked matted to her scalp and full of dirt. Most of us look the way we lived. I myself am dressed casually and am pretty clean. None of us are in the clothes we were buried in. That makes our first experiences here hard to accept as real. But no one in this crypt is making it easy on her.

"My God, she looks stank!" My friend has completely forgotten that she is not a beauty. She is here in prison orange-and-white stripes. She was killed in the laundry room when she refused to join any of the gangs. She told us that she had been short on time and was due to be released in a few weeks. Her cellmates tapped her to mail in contraband for them when she hit the ground. As a kinda mule for them. Refusal was not an option in there, I guess. Oh yeah, she was in jail for insider trading. Money ain't everything.

"Hi." She gave a little dirty smile of varying colors before adding, "My name is Lisa Gilliam. I am a crack addict."

"Hi, you old crack fiend!" The laughter started immediately after the shout-out.

"Don't laugh at me!" she screamed back at us, "Y'all are just lucky that you are further along in the program than I am!"

"Yes we are on step forty-five of six thousand!" The laughter overwhelmed everyone in the crypt except Lisa. Jonathon Brooks, whose shouts were loudest, was a child molester who was taken out by the women of the Daisy Retreat. Those witches do not play with men at all. I think they are all lesbians in disguise.

"This is serious!" she shouted, "I want to get clean by next year and get my son back."

Rollins raised his hand to stop the laughter. It didn't always work, but this time it was. She had been up here seven different times. She was eternally hooked on her last adventure.

"Okay, Lisa Gilliam, do you know where you are?"

"Yes." She spoke into the mic, still scratching and shaking, "I'm at my first N.A. meeting, right?"

"Haaaa! That's a new one on us!" Jonathon Brooks shouted. The laughter became deafening. He started to chant, "Not Alive! Not Alive!" The crowd laughed as the chant picked up. It became contagious. After a few minutes, I found myself laughing at some of the shout-outs and quick jokes.

Blam! Blam! Blam!

That shut us down. Rollins started his questioning all over again.

"Okay, Lisa Gilliam, do you know where you are?"

"Yes, I do." She looked at him and then at us, answering, "I am in a N.A. meeting with what must be the rudest people in the world."

We cheered. We have nothing else left, so why not? You can't cry once you get down here. Sadness lasts way too long.

"Okay, Lisa Gilliam, you are definitely not in the place you want to be in. Your recovery period will be the longest you've ever known in your short life."

She stood scratching for a few minutes in silence. She stared over us and through us as if it was becoming evident that we are not the people that she thought we were.

"I . . . I know I done—done some bad and horrible things in my life. But I've done a lot of good things that should weigh more than the bad stuff, right?" She looked to us and then to Rollins as she said, "I . . . I had a son. I once had a good man. I cheated on him so many times that I'm not sure if my son is his. I made bad choices. I know I've been in this room before and never kept my word on being clean and never returning. But this time . . ."

"Haaaaaaa!" The laughter from the corner crowd began to infect the room like a contagious yawn. "We have heard all that before. Why don't you find corner and watch the other NADs like we do?!"

It's the truth. She had been up there so many times that she should have realized this was a repeat of the same old messages. She had been dead for almost two years now. She was stuck in the same old drugged-out state. This is what the sadness did to a person down here. Acceptance only made this place harder to bear.

"I don't want to be like you!" she shouted at us. That was a first. "I am determined to get out of this place and get my life back!"

Sometimes some of us become a long running joke.

"I don't want to be like you!" we shouted back at her and laughed.

Blam! Blam! Blam!

Rollins stood from his chair. He raised his left arm to signify that vote was at hand.

"Everyone, now's the time to make the choice for acceptance by saying a simple yes or no." It really doesn't mean a thing. We can't get rid of anyone, but the new ones don't know that yet.

"No!" Lisa started before anyone in the crypt could say a word, "I don't want to go to jail. That place is not for crack addicts. I can't get clean in there!"

Rollins mimicked her shaking and scratching. It was the only laugh we'd gotten to enjoy in a long while. After a few minutes of laughter, Rollins motioned to the sergeant at arms.

Blam!

"Okay, we shall proceed without any further jokes." Rollins raised his left hand. Two women took Lisa by the arms and escorted her back to the unmarked section for another month of rest in her little nameless coffin. "What is your decision concerning those that stand before you? Make your choice. Make it now."

There was a resounding affirmation from the crowd. What else could we say? It's not like we could push someone back to life so they could tear up the entire system up there. It's just something to pass the long days and nights around here. We could leave the cemetery, but walking away is an adventure in never returning.

Rollins continued going through the motions of his speech, saying, "The votes are in. You can leave the stage and meet you new neighbors."

A small crowd moved up to the stage to shake hands and start talking about the lives that they once had. We got up to walk out but stopped to watch Sharon beating the crap out of her old lover with an ivory-tipped cane. By all accounts, she made her decision when she got into the car with him. That's my opinion. Take it for what it's worth. Most people don't think before they act, and they pay a heavy price.

"Come on, Clyde, let's go." Naomi pulled my arm as I stared at the fight. "It happens just about every time she sees him. It's gonna take some time for her anger to leave her. That is the hardest emotion to die out in a soul, you know." We started for the door. "Come on, I wanna talk. Come share my coffin with me?"

"I know you do. You have been talking for the past three years now."

"That's not funny. I'm a good listener!"

We laughed as we made our way past the dead oaks and freshly dug graves. There would be new arrivals before the week was out. I just hoped we could get front-row seats again.

"But this time," I told her, "we are going into my vault. The echo makes you sound a lot better."

"That's cool, 'cause talking is all we got—it does cover a bunch of dead time!"

"Girl, you are funny. That almost makes up for the no-sex-anymore thing."

11

Becoming Dad

"Hey, boy!" She kissed my forehead as she got to the table. "Good morning?"

"Hey." I had surprised her by having coffee set up on the back deck. "I figured we could sit out her for a few minutes and just enjoy the first view of the morning for a change."

"Wow, that's different for you."

"Yeah, I know it is." I handed her my journal. "I've been looking through this thing for the past two hours." I looked into her face as I admitted, "I realize how much I have changed over the years and especially over the last few months. This idea of yours has allowed me to vent without venting *on* you guys like I used to."

"I've been seeing the change for a while." She picked up the carafe and poured herself a cup of coffee before sitting back in her chair. "I'm glad it seems to have made us stronger instead of tearing us apart like most of our friends in similar circumstances."

I sat back in my chair and looked at the clouds as they moved across the morning sky. The birds seemed to start singing thirty minutes before the sun came up, and they wouldn't stop until the neighborhood started bustling too. These are things I took for granted for years.

"I realized last night at dinner that I hadn't been the man I should have been while the kids were really kids, you know?"

She glanced up at me as she flipped through the pages.

"I can understand that. We were growing up and trying to raise a family. Finances and new jobs took a toll on what was truly important."

"It was really a chore for me to start writing in that thing." I took a piece of toast and spread some jelly on it. "It took me almost a full day to write that first entry. I think it was close to five when I finished. I had already started cooking dinner for you guys. I think y'all hated my pork chops, but you didn't say a thing."

"I remember that day." She sipped her coffee. "No comment."

We laughed. This had become a regular thing between us. We laugh together more often than we did before I lost my job. Back then, I was all work and no fun. I know that now. All the fun we ever used to have together as a family was either forced or an over-scheduled vacation. Overtime was my first love. I took all I could and looked for ways to be away from home so as to make more money.

"I really want you to look through it. I want to find out if you see the things in me that I hope are gone."

"You sure? This is supposed to be for your eyes only."

"Yeah, I am. I heard an old family conference recording by Tony Evans the other morning, and it struck a nerve in me." I looked into her eyes, saying, "I want you to know my every thought and emotion. Hell, we've been married for eighteen years, so why not? I have nothing to hide from you."

"I know. I checked."

We laughed. She flicked through the pages and checked her watch.

"I do have to go to work in an hour. Is this why you set the alarm early?"

"Yes and no. I was going to surprise you with breakfast in bed, but you know what happened the last time I tried that."

"Can't forget it."

"Overlook my bad handwriting, okay?"

We laughed again as she began to read the first page aloud. I was nervous when she started, but I began feel at ease as I listened to my words in her voice.

Day 1
Journal Entry: A New Day?

This will be my first entry into this journal. I am neither proud nor happy to be following the advice of my wife, but I can't let the anger over my job contaminate my house any longer. Honey wants me to document the changes that will take place in me over the upcoming weeks. This will be short. I will find a job within a few weeks. I am guessing three at the most.

Okay, the emotional part of this is that I am pissed off. Twenty-five years at the same company, just to be forced into retirement by a buyout? I am forty-six years old, how in the world can I start over now? My words are DAMN! And HELL!

I made dinner. I smothered pork chops, and they came out tough as leather. I used to cook so good that they would always ask when I would cook again. They ate it all. No one complained. They didn't ask for seconds. I know that they didn't like it. I didn't like it.

All I could do was look at her as she read and watch her mouth form my old words. All of the time that had passed had made me realize how much she and I fit with each other.

"Well, you want me to continue?" She smiled, saying, "This has intrigued my curiosities into what you were thinking each time you opened up." She started thumbing through the pages again. "Okay, let's look at this one. The title caught my eye."

Day 39
Journal Entry: Better Than Me

I am both happy and mad. Honey has accomplished what she's been working on these past three years. She has landed the promotion to Department Head. I am proud of her, but I do feel that my manhood may be in jeopardy. My wife is making more money than I am. I am still without a job.

I am the one doing the household chores now. I am the one cooking and making sure the kids are off to school. What a reversal of fortune. I can't be disappointed. I am grateful that she is mine and I am hers.

Pissed is what I am with myself. I should have followed her lead. I should have gone back to school to add to my resume. Twenty-five years of experience doesn't matter in this day and age. Hindsight--damn . . .

"Wow, I didn't know you felt that way." She scanned through a few more pages. "Hold on for a second." She got up and walked away, dialing. "Hey Jane, I'll be a little late this morning. Let's say about ten. I have some things going on I can't get away from this morning." She looked at me before adding, "Yeah, it is very important that I be home with my family, so I will be in by ten."

She hung up the phone and came back to the deck chair beside me.

"I called Jane to let her know we need a little more time here."

"I'm so glad you're the boss."

"I am too." She smiled at me. "But you are my boss and I do feel that we should be here for each other. This opportunity will not come up again, so I figured I'd take advantage of it and you."

"Oh yeah?"

"Yeah."

She opened the journal and started flipping the pages again. I started holding onto a nervous happy feeling, you know? This was all still part of me growing up. She was the best person I knew, and a woman who could handle change and still keep pushing forward.

"I think I found the next one."

DAY 153
Journal Entry: Summers Are Way Too Long

I am bored to tears. I have now been turned down for thirty-two different jobs. I am either overqualified or they tell me I don't have the right experience. I am still stuck with the question of why they schedule interviews when they know who they want to fill the position? It is still such a who-you-know type of thing.

My children are driving me crazy. I have gone to the mall more times in the past three weeks than I have in the past ten years. The girls have worn me thin with taking them and their friends back and forth from softball practices, dance rehearsals, and trips to the movies. But such is life. I should have grabbed me a hobby instead of working and watching other grown men play children's games.

I do wish Chad was older. An eight-year-old just can't understand the essence of a good light heavyweight fight. But he is the man. I watched his little basketball game this afternoon--he was all over the court. He's actually pretty good. I have been missing my son develop.

But in the interim, I just want a few hours of quiet. My kids talk way too much, especially early in the morning. I think that is supposed to be my time, because when they are with their friends, our conversations are limited to "Take us here!" and "Can you give me a few more dollars?"

I am seeing what Honey had been saying for years. I need to apologize to her. I used to think that she was just exaggerating about how hard it was to keep up with the kids.

"Okay, I'm waiting," she said as she smiled over the page.

"Waiting? For what, may I ask?"

"The apology you owe me for all the times you thought I was just making small talk about how difficult it is being the kid's servant and confidant."

"I truly apologize for thinking that your kids weren't that bad."

"My kids?" We laughed. "You had a hand in this mess, mister."

I heard the rattling of glasses in the dishwasher and the muffled talk of my little pains. The door opened, and out walked all three of them. Smiling at the both of us like they hit the jackpot.

"Hey, this is cool!" Janice pulled up a chair and sat down. "We haven't eaten out here in years. What's the occasion?"

"Yeah, what's the occasion?" Chad sat on the step and gulped down some juice.

"There is no occasion. We were just out here talking and thinking about the family and our life together."

"Mom, are you guys having problems?"

"Eron, why would you ask us something like that?"

"Well, it's been a long time since Dad worked, and we talked about this last week—about how you guys have been laughing and playing around with each other at dinner and stuff like that. That's a sign of family problems, right?" she asked.

"Where did y'all get that mess from?"

"Well, we were watching a movie on Lifetime and the parents were all cuddly then the wife slapped the dad with divorce papers and married a younger guy." The girls buttered their toast like the conversation was matter-of-fact, explaining, "We just wanted the right time to ask."

"Well, the answer is no. I would have to kill some young guy trying to court the love of my life!" Honey smiled at me. "We don't have any major problems. The house is paid off and the bills are not overdue. We are fine. Matter of fact, I am enjoying you guys. I am learning a lot about myself through the things that we all talk about and the things that you guys do away from the house."

"Dad, are you in therapy or something?"

"No, I am not!" We all laughed. "I am not losing my mind. I kind of like being at home, but it is a change from all the hours and days I used to spend at work."

"I liked it when you came to my basketball game."

"Thanks, Chad." He made me feel good, and I told him so, "I really liked being there.

"Well, what are you guys doing out here? Are we interrupting a romantic moment?"

"I do sometimes forget that you girls are teens now." Honey opened the journal and started thumbing through it again. "We were just discussing some of the events of this last year. Do you want to hear one of them?"

"Yeah, that'll be cool!"

"Okay . . ."

DAY 93
Journal Entry: The Intruder

My day did start out okay. As any other, I made breakfast for everyone, made the beds, and cut the grass in the backyard before lunch. I thought I would have time to sit and relax before I had to get dinner ready.

It wasn't until 10:30 that my whole world changed. The school called about Eron's little intruder at the school. How does a dad deal with his daughter's first cycle? I really wasn't expecting this to happen on my time. I missed out on Janice's visitor's first time, because of course I was at work. The conversation in the car was too strange. She looked at me like I had mud on my face, or was she taking pity on me?

I might have overdone it at the store with all the purchases I made. In a way, it was proactive on my part to pick up enough supplies to last her for at least a year and a half. Honey laughed for what seemed like hours. I didn't think that she would call my T-Jones and discuss it. Today was a change in my mind, and Eron's for sure.

"Oh my god!" My daughter would get overly excited over things sometimes. "Dad, you wrote that about me? In there . . . ? Who else has seen this?!" She put her glass down, exclaiming all over again, "Oh my god!"

"Girl, no one else has seen or read this."

"Eron, did the police go to your school about the intruder? Were there TV cameras there?"

"Chad, grow up! Mom, *please* tear it out of there!"

"Oh, this is good. I will cherish this one for Thanksgiving." We laughed, but Eron refused to see the humor. "Everyone is coming here for dinner, so we will just have to put copies of this page out for placemats."

"Come on! Why is my life so funny all of a sudden?"

"What's funny about an intruder at school? Was it one of those Internet guys?"

"Chad, we will have a talk about this later this afternoon, okay?"

"Sure, Dad."

"Y'all finish eating and go get ready for school."

"Okay, Dad," they said, not moving to get up, "Mom, read one more. We have time!"

Honey looked at me and turned a few pages.

DAY 101
Journal Entry: Time Is My Enemy!

I felt pretty good today. I sat in a hot tub of water and relaxed. My problem was that I relaxed for way too long. I forgot that school was supposed to let out early today. Eron, Janice, and their friends were in the living room talking loudly before I realized my mistake. They were having teen conversations about boys and who in the neighborhood was fine. They switched from boys to men. I listened kinda hard. I made their friends' list. I smiled like a Cheshire cat.

I kept smiling until I looked in the mirror. It made me wonder why Honey still looks at me as if I am twenty-five and healthy. I am sporting a three pack and love handles that resemble elf shoes, and my pecs look like tiny fallen boobs.

I stayed to stare at my reflection for too long. Eron and her friends walked in my room and saw me in my Batman boxers. I couldn't move to the closet fast enough.

Time is not my friend.

I am working out starting tomorrow!

The laughter that filled the backyard scared the birds away. Chad kept telling me that he didn't know I'd kept the boxers he had given me for Christmas as a joke. Honey closed the journal and put her coffee down, unable to control herself. The girls had vindication for all the times I had embarrassed them at the mall by dancing around the van to open doors for their little troupe. Truly what you give, you get back in return. I joined in the laughter.

"Okay, it *is* funny," I stood up and flexed my muscles for them, "but it's not that funny. I'm in good shape now!" They didn't stop. I think I fueled the fires. "I am in shape. I have been working out four days a week since then."

"We know," they snorted as they kept laughing, "because we hear you grunting while you are trying to find the Hulk inside that old frame."

"Honey, you to?"

"Alright, alright!" I had to put things back into perspective. "Finish eating and get dressed! Time is fading, and we got to get into the routine of the day."

"Okay, Batman!" Chad got one in on me.

"That's a good one, Chad!" His sisters hi-fived him as they drank down the remains of their juice and took their toast and orange slices into the house. Eron seemed to feel a great deal better as she turned to tell me, "Watch for the signal, we will be ready then!"

"Funny. Very funny."

They left. Honey looked at me. Her cheeks were red and eyes were watering.

"This was a good morning." She handed me back the journal. "Thank you for allowing us to see that side of you."

"I am glad that things happened the way they did," I answered as I drank my coffee, "This has shown me that I was not really at my full potential as a father and a husband to you."

"You don't have to say that. You have always done your best for us." She grabbed my hand as she led me down the stairs. "You stood by me and talked me into going back to school. You listened to me fuss about the buttheads I've worked with over the past ten years. I want to thank you for that." She kissed me. I felt renewed. "This is a time that you don't have to rush. We are in a good place, okay?"

"I can't quite see it." I squeezed her hand as she got to the driver's side of the car. "I will be better. I do love you guys."

"You show it all the time and don't realize it. All the crazy stuff you have done leaves memories that can't be replaced or turned away from the way you have loved us over the years. Today, you just sealed our love for you a little more. Not a lot of dads would allow their kids to see them in their Batman underwear."

"They were boxers!"

She got into the car. I handed her the cell phone. She dropped it in her purse.

"Look, we have very few bills. It was a good decision to use your retirement package to pay off the house. You assured that we'll have a roof over our heads. That was a dad-type of thing. I can't fault you for that. You take care of us. I love you for that, as well as for your love handles and that newly reappearing six-pack. I feel so lucky that we have made it this far."

"You are lucky. Hell, I am too. You could have chosen anyone, but you decided to stick with me."

She started the car.

"We work well together. Don't forget that."

I closed the door and watched her back out of the drive. I stood there for a few seconds to get myself together. I turned to walk toward the backyard and was surprised by some new super-villains.

"Batman, we know your secret. You are doomed!" Chad hit me in the face with a water balloon as he shouted his rant, "Doomed, I tell you!" The ice-cold water burst over me as the barrage of water balloons continued. "Doomed, I tell you!"

"You better run!" I shouted back at them. I ran into the backyard as my neighbor Jayson came out to leave for work. I ignored his wave to chase after my kids, laughing.

12
Love of the Game

THIS HAS BEEN ONE THE PROUDEST DAYS OF MY LIFE. ALL THESE people came out to see the woman I married. I think it was more than have ever come out before. I am proud of her and I love her for what she represents—true and determined love.

I sat back in my chair as the people filed by to look at her. They left the small white-and-pink handkerchiefs she asked to be used in place of the customary flowers at an occasion such as this. She didn't want anyone to shed a tear over her going home. The bright lights in here gave her skin a heavenly glow. I looked at her in that box. My mind went over the last words I head her say to me, "I am glad that we were us." They did a good job on her makeup. The battle to live just a few days longer than the doctors expected had taken a great deal of her natural beauty. She impressed us all by making it two years past the date they gave her. She was still a beauty.

I saw so many that I knew and a great many who I had only seen on television. She impacted them all. I had been sitting here for more than four hours. Shaking hands and taking in their greetings and condolences. I had let the grief leave me days ago, when she told me that she couldn't see a way to fight any longer. She asked me to forgive her for tiring so suddenly. That last kiss—our last time holding hands—made all the times we had talked and laughed together seem like a childhood memory. I said goodbye to my love three days ago. Now it is their turn. They loved her too.

"Amazing Grace . . . " The pastor spoke slowly to begin the service, ". . . that saved a wretch like me." The crowd of people took their seats and stopped talking to listen as the pastor began, "Good afternoon, my brothers and my sisters."

"Good afternoon!" they answered

"We are here to celebrate the home-going of our beloved sister, Connie 'The Game' Chesney."

The cheers rose slowly but soon became overwhelming. I let the tears fall from my eyes. I didn't want to hold back, as I had promised her that I would not. It took a few minutes for the crowd to settle. The settling silence opened the door to the reality of my wife not being around after today. All I could think was that this was a home-going for a person who truly didn't deserve to die.

I sat there and watched all the grieving people I didn't know, though the world knew because of their social status, but I couldn't really see them. I kept falling back into memories of first dates, first kisses, first fusses, broken dishes, and the first time she saw her hair falling out in clumps from the treatments for the bone cancer that had taken her from me. I watched as the life walked out of her eyes. I watched the joy of living turn into a true struggle to try and make me happy. I just wanted her to live with me until we grew too old to get out of bed. I felt cheated . . .

After about an hour of guest speakers' words of condolence, I had my turn at the podium.

"Hello everyone . . . " I had to clear my throat several times. It felt as if I had a piece of sand stuck in it. "I am Clarence Chesney. I am Connie Chesney's husband." I motioned for the projectionist to begin the slideshow as I talked, "I don't have a great deal to say. I have promised to read the words of my friend to you on this day. I am glad that you all have come and supported me through this terrible day in my life. Today feels far more tragic than the day we first got word that her time was limited. But she didn't fail to surprise me—and, I'm sure, all of you—with her strength and determination.

"I have not rehearsed this, so I really don't know what she has written. She asked me to keep this letter closed until it was my turn to speak. These are the words of my friend, lover, partner, wife . . . my life."

This is a day that I didn't want to take place. I have realized that in my life I have had the opportunity to make some people hate me and some people love me to the extent that I kept pushing myself even when the pain would make the silent tears fall because no sound could compare to what I was feeling.

I want to thank all of you for showing up to my home-going. I want to thank the women of the Daisy Retreat for helping me find myself and leave the past behind. This is not a funeral. I am poised to meet our Heavenly Father and wait for my loving husband. I only ask that you guys check on him from time to time because he does not cook well and I don't want some sorry woman to get my husband while he is down and missing me. I want to be selfish and ask that he be alone for his remaining years, because I don't want our love to ever fade.

I also want to thank the NBA for allowing me to fulfill a dream that has been the dream of so many women who were probably better ball players than I could have ever been. I want to tell those of you who are suffering a similar fate--those of you who are battling cancer--don't quit, don't ever give up just for the sake of giving up.

I realize that we all have struggles and have all fallen on our faces from time to time, but don't quit on yourselves. The moment you decide to give up, that's the moment you were supposed to help someone else out of their own struggles. I often think about all the hospitals I visited and the people I have met there who went home before I did; they all kept me feeling encouraged even as I tried to encourage them.

Life is not fair or forgiving. Life is what it is intended to be: LIVED! So leave here today and know that I lived my life. I have loved a good man. I have made good friends. I have fought the good fight. I am ready for the next life, the eternal life.

I will always love you, Clarence. Now stop crying and play the tape.

"I don't think I was supposed to read the last part." I smiled as the crowd laughed softly along with me. "She had an extra note under that."

I motioned for them to play the video as I made my way back to my seat. The lights went dim. The crowd in the video was lively and screaming. The sound of Marv Albert's voice over the cheering crowd took me back to that night:

"Folks, it started two years ago with one letter, determination, and a whole lot of love. For those of you who don't already know the story of Connie 'The Game' Chesney, I'll tell her inspiring history again. This is a story you can't get tired of hearing.

"It has been a three-year struggle for this thirty-five-year-old woman and her devoted husband. The Game was diagnosed with bone sarcoma and wasn't expected to survive more than eight months.

"Empowered by her love for this game and assisted every step of the way by her loving husband Clarence, The Game continued to watch her Dallas Mavericks in the same seats that she had held for the past fifteen years. Her intimate knowledge of this team and her joy in the game gave her husband the idea of soliciting help from the Make-A-Wish Foundation to make the strange request to the Dallas Mavericks. The request allowed The Game to become a member of the team for three days—for one game—for one shot to fulfill her dream of playing in the NBA.

"Stranger than fiction, the story soon took on a life of its own. After her first appearance on the court last November, requests poured in from across the nation to the NBA Commissioner's office for Mrs. Chesney to become the only player in NBA history to not only play for every team, but score in all the games she played in. From then on, The Game was truly on. In every game she's played, the team that had her as a three-day guest on the roster has won.

"Either she's incredibly lucky, or her determination is moving enough to keep inspiring last-place teams to overwhelm first-ranked teams by twenty points or more. Following the Commissioner's ruling, each team had to agree to drop one player from its active roster in order for her to pick up a three-day contract. Every team has agreed to the deal, with some top players even asking to donate their spots on the roster.

"Her health is not what it was when this trek began. She has proved that a strong will, pure passion, and sheer determination can give rise to incredible accomplishments in spite of any circumstance. We are all here on this night to watch what could be a truly historic moment. This moment could inspire all of us to look at life a little differently. It should show us that if we all reach out to help one, we can truly help many.

"If we look at her now, The Game doesn't stand as upright as she did some months ago. Her hair is gone due to the side effects of the treatments she has had to endure during her quest to complete this dream, but so far she's continued to fend off the enemy that has been trying to destroy her insurmountable spirit. We have been informed by team doctors that she may not be able to do what is expected of her, but she is refusing to accept their diagnosis.

"The teams are coming to the floor. It's getting so loud in here that I doubt you will be able to hear me. There she is. Connie 'The Game' Chesney. She has been described as the most educated fan in NBA history. She can quote stats from games that most of us have completely forgotten about. She has been both loved by many and ridiculed by some as recently as last week for, and I quote, 'performing for sympathy.' In response to these criticisms, she has only said that basketball has been the love of her life, second only to her husband, who has kept her going in pursuit of her dreams.

"Let's focus on the floor. Both teams have waived the customary introductions in hopes that The Game will have enough strength to complete her task. She is undoubtedly in pain. But there she is, ready to make the final shot in her NBA career.

"There's the tip-off. The pass goes to The Game. She dribbles and backs away from her patented three-foot jumper. She has moved to the top of the key. Folks, the players on the floor have moved away to watch her shoot. This is not only chivalric, but something for the history books. Love does seem to conquer all . . .

"She stops! She shoots! Oh Lawd! Oh Lawd! She made it! This crowd is erupting. It's so loud in here that I can't hear what my director is saying in my ear . . . Oh Lawd! I'm floored by the strength it must have taken her to make that shot. The players have cleared the benches. They are lining up to shake her hand while two players lift her up in this moment of triumph.

"This is her moment!" a fan shouted in the announcer's mic, "This is her moment!"

"I am overwhelmed with the sheer emotion of this moment. Let's look at the replay. Cue it up, boys. Look, right after her release, she points to her husband, who has always sat courtside to cheer for her. This has been a good career. Her career hasn't been about money or glory. Instead, it has been about bringing attention to the battle so many fight through on a daily basis. Tonight has been a good night.

"Ladies and gentlemen, I love this game!"

The video skipped back to her jump shot. It stopped on her release of the ball. The caption under her feet simply read, "We Love The Game!" Everyone stood and gave her one final ovation. It lasted for what must have been five full minutes. They loved her as much as I still do.

All I can say to all of this is . . . I am still in love with Connie.

13
Penelope's Peril

Shree Boomp! Shree Boomp! Shree Boomp! The streets were still holding onto the morning dewdrops. They looked like they had been crying all night to try and relieve the pangs of the upcoming hustle and bustle of the day.

The tires agreed with the road as we drove: *Shree Boomp! Shree Boomp! Shree Boomp!* It dawned on me that these same roads were screaming jokes at me. Laughing at me because of the loss in my family.

Shree Boomp! I wanted to scream.

Shree Boomp! Everybody in the family car, crying and adding weight to the pressures I had been holding in for days.

Shree Boomp! Shree Boomp! Shree Boomp! I just knew it was the universe laughing at me through the road. *He's dead! He's dead!* Tormenting me. Tormenting me enough that I wanted to shout at Mother for sitting there so quietly while she turned through the small book of photos she hadn't stopped looking at for the past three days.

Shree Boomp! Shree Boomp! Shree Boomp! My heart hurt all over again as their words reminded me that my dad had gone home.

He's dead! He's dead! I had begun to hate this morning's commute. *Shree Boomp! Shree Boomp! Shree Boomp!* I felt like I was in a hole, looking up with no way out.

The limo pulled up to the church too slowly for my comfort. This was the day I had been dreading for the past four weeks. Daddy was only trying to regain what was taken from me. He was just not as quick as he used to be. Stanley Franklin got lucky. I think if he hadn't had the opportunity to find that broken pipe, Daddy would've beaten the hell out of him before the cops got there. Maybe we just didn't call the cops in time . . .

The car stopped. The funeral director got out and opened the door for us.

"This will be the last time I ever come to this church," I mumbled as I stepped out of the death-car. I wasn't speaking loudly enough for anyone to care, "I hate this church. I hate this building. I hate this entire block. I hate that Dad had to die."

The walk into the church was the longest in my life. Even the days of visiting Daddy in the hospital were not as ghoulish as this one. I looked up at the sky and wondered why rain clouds were not visible overhead. Even the clouds had no respect for my father. I felt a little better after leaving the sounds of that death-car behind.

My heart dropped as I entered the church. My eyes ran across the pews. I counted fifty-six. We were ushered into the first pew. Then I felt the crush of pain all over again as they positioned the casket in the front aisle of the church, just below the pulpit. Even though it was a new casket, I knew I heard the hinges tell me that the first man to love me was gone for good. Mother, Sabrina, Sarah, and Doug hadn't stopped their crying since we got into the limo. Me, I let my mind drift so the tears would not find their way out.

My mind raced back over the countless hours of prayers, pleading, and begging for my father to remain here with us for a few more years. No answer. No respect.

Pilgrim's Rest had not changed in the thirteen years we had been coming here. As I looked down at that same stank dark red carpet, I realized how I hated this church. I hated the pews. I hated the fake chandeliers. I hated the pictures of the little white Jesus they had hanging all over the place.

"Why haven't they changed the color of this carpet in all these years?" I whispered to my mother.

Damn! Oh well, I cursed in church. It wasn't the worst I had heard in here, especially after business meetings.

We were seated. I sat as still as I could as the others filed in behind our little procession. I purposely ignored their crying. I focused on the box that held what was left of my father. I watched as the young funeral director placed the wreaths, flowers, and signs around it. As he his fumbling knocked over the framed portrait he had just finished arranging, I thought to myself, *Sorry-butt moron.*

Click! Click! Click! The box shouted at us to pay attention. *Click! Click! Click!*

They locked the wheels in place. The lid was opened. I stood to look in. I didn't remember walking over, but found myself being held by my mother as I stared at the makeup someone had smeared on his face. I stood there and felt my anger surge beyond my limits. I knew now what I had to do to make this right for my father's sake—for my family's sake.

"Penelope?" Mother spoke to me in a loving tone.

"Hell has no fury like a woman scorned," I whispered to my father, "I will burn him for you." I stood up slowly and looked at her.

"Penelope, did you say something?" Mother whispered to me, but I refused to answer.

"Come on Penelope, I know this is hard. He loved us a lot."

"I know," I did not let a tear fall as I struggled to say, "He shoulda just counted like he'd been telling us to do all of these years:

'Count to three and gain control before your act.' But he didn't do that, did he?"

"He did count." She looked in the box and kept trying to explain to me things I already knew, "What happened to you cut him too deep. I never saw him so angry in the twenty-five years I have known him."

"This was not his fault," I whispered fiercely.

"He knew that. He just wanted to rectify the situation by hurting Stanley as bad as he hurt you and all of us. Stanley destroyed our trust and all the love we had for him." She gasped and took a deep breath before going on, "If I were six years younger and just a little in shape, I would poison him or beat his ass like a man." She looked at me and said seriously, "He took my heart. I do wish God gives him his just due."

"Momma?" I looked back into the box.

"Yes, baby?"

"I thought you told me that I was your heart." I forced a smile passed my anger.

"Girl, you are your father's child." We hugged and sat back down.

I didn't listen to the two singers, to the preacher, or my dad's ten co-workers, who all seemed to say the exact same things. Things I had always known about him. I didn't listen to the four cousins who handed my mother envelopes with money in them. They had owed my dad for years, and this is the moment they choose to pay it back. He would help anybody and never fussed about the money. He would just say, "It's about the fellowship." This was the important part of his friendship with his family. He explained it to me when I was thirteen: "If people don't pay you back or share fellowship with you after they have taken funds from you, they don't care a thing about you." I got lost in my memories of our old conversation and missed several people talk about his army days. Then came the letter he always told us he would want read at the end of his funeral. I had thought it was just one of his jokes.

"Mom, is this for real?" my brother asked.

Planting Daisies

Mother just smiled and sat there shaking her head. I let a smile cross my lips as I looked at the preacher, who had no clue what he was getting himself into.

"Mom!" my sisters whispered loudly, "Stop this!"

"He had one request for his children and wife . . ." Reverend Mike looked at all of us.

My sisters looked at me. I looked at my brother. They were all in shock. I gave them the best cheesy smile I could muster. The tears had gone. The embarrassment took over. Dad was in the room, making things better like he always had by doing something out of the ordinary to comfort us. The hardened and beaten faces looked soft again.

"Come on, family. In his letter, he said, 'Don't let them sit there. Call them out and call them out loudly.'" He raised the letter up. "To use his exact words, 'Don't let them sit there . . .'"

We joined in, ". . . too cotton-pickin' long!" We laughed. Everyone that knew him knew he used that phrase too often.

Mother was the first to stand up. She walked over to the box, looked in, and shook her heard. Smiling the entire time, she motioned for us to join her in the moment of embarrassment. We moved hesitantly. I walked over and took two of the four microphones. I handed one to Mother and stood in silence as my brothers and sisters retrieved mics for themselves. I found comfort in thinking how much time my non-singing father had spent singing to us. My family stood in silence, glancing at each other with "I am *not* going first," written all over each of our faces.

I smiled.

I took a deep breath.

"*I got a good-looking daddy!*" I sang out in my best Patti La-Belle voice. I hammed it up, "*I uh I uh I got a gooooooood loooooking da–uh–daddy . . . And there is not a man . . . I said . . . there is not a man that looks better than him!*"

I closed my eyes and started all over again. It hurt like hell. I knew Dad would be proud of me. Mother joined in. Sarah and Sabrina sang, but they didn't get into it like Mother and me. Doug added a beatbox that got the church clapping.

"*I got a good-looking daddy!*"

We sang for a few more minutes, stopping to a standing ovation. For those few minutes, the pain had left us. I could feel the love for my dad in the way we sang and smiled. Our cousins joined us, and the tempo of the song changed again. The clapping and singing was the best send-off we could have given him.

———

That was three years ago.

The memory of anger was still so real that I couldn't focus on what I was doing. Stanley Franklin raped me, lied to my family, and took my father away from us. Three years had come and gone. Three years had not taken the strength of the memory away from me. I still hurt. So they will continue to hurt.

"Good morning, this is Darian Ward reporting to you from the site of another discovery. Police still don't have a clue how many more bodies they might find in this four mile stretch." The camera panned to the woods. I perked up. I wanted to see if the clue I had left would still be on the tree. "By all accounts, this is the twentieth victim to be discovered in the past two years. The question is still open as to whether a vigilante may be murdering random people or whether there could be some kind of connection between all the people who have lost their lives this way. The FBI has compiled a list of the murder victims and said in a recent press conference that they are all on the Sexual Offender Registry. This alone should strike fear into the public, but as always, there are those who think these deaths are less than tragic. I had the opportunity to talk with one onlooker . . . "

I didn't pay attention to a word he said. I looked for the tree and saw that the clue was still hanging there. It seemed so obvious, but maybe just to me. I felt joy overtake my heart knowing that Darian Ward would be back out in a few days to report on the same old thing. The only difference would be the location.

I didn't watch the rest of the news. I had to get to class and turn in my work. I had to keep up appearances. Three hours of sleep, but I felt good. I had to stop by the Daisy Retreat and make a showing at self-defense class, get groceries, and wash my car.

The day had already been too long when I found myself at my friend Lyrix's apartment, surrounded by witnesses. I loved 'em to death, but they were sucking my glow out. So I would keep my mask on.

"Hey, girls!" Doobie came in. Late, as usual. "How's school, Penelope?"

"It's okay. Just trying to stay on the dean's list for this semester."

"Again?" Kyra shouted from the kitchen, "You are always on your game at the head of the class. You've been doing that since Filmore Junior High!"

"Hush, y'all, and deal the cards," Lyrix said while pouring soda into her glass. "We all know she is smart as anything, but she can't play spades worth a damn."

"Lyrix, you know we have been taking it easy on you guys." I always play as Dana's partner. "Penny, whoop their asses again."

"Again? Y'all only beat us twice last month, and that was a fluke."

"Fluke? Fluke?! Lyrix, I think you need to get a man so you can think a little better than you have been." Everyone laughed. "You need someone to come in here and change your oil on the regular."

"The regular!" We laughed in stereo.

Like I said, I loved these women. We had all been through some of the same experiences, or we know people who had. I still couldn't get my latest conquest off my mind. I smiled at the silly jokes, sipped a little wine, played to win the game, cheated a little to help things go our way, and weighed in with a few comments here and there. None of them knew how mad I still got at just the thought of Stanley Franklin still living and breathing. In between games, I pulled out my cell to check my streaming video.

"Girl, who are you texting so much?" Dana asked, nosey thing that she was.

"I'm not texting—just checking my email for a grade to come in from one of my professors." I gave a fake smile before adding, "Like I have time for any man to be in my life right now! I'm no Jody Whatley. I am not looking for a new love."

I went back to my phone and let them continue to talk about men and the meaning of that song. I was watching the link I had set up in my dad's tree house, where I had placed Mr. Neal Douglass. I saw his ass was awake, screaming and crying like a little girl. I so wanted to turn the sound up. My hands started to shake, but I knew the explanation would only lead them to tell Carron about my activities, and she would have to arrest me. But that's what you get for having a friend that's a cop.

"Penelope? Penelope!" I was lost in the daydream. I heard them calling me, but it was just a game. It was just hard to break my attention away from the phone.

"Girl, come on." Dana was excited. That was always her flaw in playing any type of game. She allowed her emotions to show what she was about to do. If we were playing poker, I would clean them out again. "I am ready to have some other butts in these seats."

"Okay, okay." I took one last look and punched in the codes that would set off the electronics before I returned to confront Mr. Douglass for his crimes. "Girl, my hand is subpar. I can only get four or five." I was lying. I had six high spades in my hand and two jokers.

"See, that's it. That's it." Doobie never knew when to keep her mouth shut. "They're gonna win again. Y'all know Penelope is cold and calculating. That's why she wins at poker all the time. She's the type that could probably could kill a man and never get caught."

They laughed. My heart dropped. I only snickered. With twenty-six of them gone, I was still winning.

We played for hours, laughed about old jokes that we rolled on years ago, talked about old boyfriends, frozen TV-dinners, broken hearts, revenge, and the constant talk over the news stories about those missing sex offenders. I only listened and enjoyed their conversations about the killer dealing death to rapists guilty of killing off part of the people they had violated. Man or woman, they deserved what they got.

Talk went on and on about the bodies and how the killer might be a member of the Daisy Retreat. That idea was blown off. The members of the Retreat would never go to that extreme, or give rapists such an escape from the pain of life. They only built self-esteem and new lives for rape victims.

"Okay y'all, that's game again." We had won again. Dana was happy for a change. "Next!"

I smiled at her.

"That's six in a row." I pushed the cards to the middle of the table. "I'm done." I had to keep up the role of the good student, so I said, "We'll beat you guys up again next time."

"Girl, it's Friday night and two in the morning. What are we gonna do now?"

That was my clue to leave and get to work. Carron walked in and smiled at everyone before calling Lyrix over. They whispered and laughed for a few minutes.

"I'm bailing on you guys. I've got a paper I want to get done so I can turn it in early ... "

They all completed my sentence for me: "Hahaha, y'all know I wanna get the top spot at graduation. So it's all work and no play for this girl."

There was a knock at the door, Carron opened it and introduced Jayson to everyone. I shook his hand and looked into his eyes to see if he would fit for one of my conquests. He had calm eyes. I couldn't get a bead on him, so I grabbed my bag and headed out the door. I was followed by four of the twelve women at the party. We all tended to walk one another to our cars when we left. Never going alone was always a good thing. But even in big numbers, I still felt alone.

The two-hour drive was nice and quiet. I only passed four cars on my way to the tree house. I listened to a tape of Lois Alba, Dinah Washington, and Phyllis Hyman to get me in the mood to confront Mr. Douglass and make up my mind on how he would meet his end.

I had already emptied his bank account and cashed out his 401K. The majority of the funds would arrive at the Daisy Retreats in Ontario and Fairfax in a week or so. His suicide should look altruistic. But that would depend on his nature and whether he wanted to put up a fight.

Squump! Squump! Squump!

The sound of plastic under boots always makes the strangest sounds. It warmed my heart.

"Well, hello Mr. Douglass." His eyes popped open. "How have you been doing?"

His garbled speech tickled me.

"Ssshhh!" I leaned close to his ear to whisper, "I know it hurts. The pressure on your wrists has got to be driving you crazy, huh?"

"It hurts like hell!"

I watched the tears leave his bloodshot eyes and roll down his cheek. "Why me?" he asked. He took a big breath. "I don't know you. I haven't done a thing to you." He took another big breath, begging, "Why me?"

"Why not you?" I spoke to him in the slowest cadence I could, "What about the little boys that you violated and ruined?"

"I keep telling everybody that was not me! I promise you that it was not me!" He was talking fast. I put it down to the fact that the bottoms of his ankles and wrists were slowly being crushed by the vise they were placed in. "Why are you hiding your face? I didn't hurt you! I didn't hurt you!" He was grasping for straws and thinking revenge in the wrong way. "It wasn't me!" He opened his eyes and looked at me. "It was my brother."

Well, that threw me off for a few seconds. Then I realized . . . *He must have watched!*

"What is your brother's name, and where can I find him?"

"Stop doing what you are doing to me and I'll tell you anything you want."

"Okay, I can do that." I smiled from under my orange-colored mask. "Hold on for one second." I turned off my little contraption crushing his wrists and ankles. I took out my largest pair of wire cutters and cut off his pinky toe.

"OOOOWWW!" He grunted for a few minutes, gasping, "You sorry mother . . . " I cut him off.

"Oh, shut up!" I laughed because his crying was funny. "It's only the tip of the dang thing anyway. So stop crying like a little girl." I couldn't contain my smile. "Now, how did you help your brother and where is he?"

"My brother . . . " he sniffled as he started crying all over again.

Some men cannot take any type of pain. Good thing they don't have to bear children.

"Look, you're wasting my time. I need names and addresses. You clowns never operate alone." I placed a smaller pair of wire cutters on his leg as I said in my most intimidating tone, "Speak!" It was just a distraction though. I was going to lay his ass bare.

He started talking, spilling out names and addresses that seemed to kindle the anger that had always been in me. I still had seven hours of record time not used. I knew I could take my time. I never kept souvenirs, but I did know that the FBI or whoever else would be trying to breakdown the videos I'd filmed would see that they are sweet and generic. I had added recorded background noises from remote areas that would take them quite a while to figure out. All the clues would lead them to the conclusion that it was a team of men acting out on these freaks.

After an hour of listening to his stories and weak excuses, my anger had reached a fever pitch. I kept my back to the camera. I made motions like my right leg was injured and walked around the little table Mr. Douglass was strapped to. I moved several objects in view of the camera. I shut the camera lens and left it running. The voice modulation added weight to the last words Mr. Douglass heard as a breathing pedophile. There were screams upon screams. They didn't bother me too much—the ear plugs blocked a lot of them out. Besides, the cracking of crushing bones made me think of playing dominoes with my dad and brother.

"Mr. Douglass!" I shouted at him, "Look at me. It's time for you to go."

"Thank you." His groggy eyes opened in relief for the last time to say, "I am sorry for ever allowing these things to happen. Thank you for listening." He smiled. "I can go on without this weight on me anymore."

"I am the wrong person to apologize to."

I pressed the off button on the remote, killing the camera. I stepped back and watched the flow of blood from the openings in his thighs. A heart can't pump for long without a good supply of blood. Sleep accepted him for the last time.

Meep! Meep! Meep!

"Oh, wow," I rolled over and looked at the sun breaking through the blinds. "It's morning already?" I turned the alarm off and turned on the TV. Channel 14 News was brighter and bolder that ever on the new set. Hooray!

"We are reporting this morning from Maplewood, where yet another body has been discovered. If you would look behind me toward the tree line and at the bottom of the hill, you will see the flashing lights of police cars. From all the information coming in, we can say that the victim was a young woman. The scramble for information has investigators wondering if this latest find could be related to the group that appears to be targeting pedophiles residing in and around our broadcast area."

"That's right! That's right!" a bystander screamed from behind Sheila, who always seemed to be having a bad hair day, "Kill all them baby-raping clowns!" Others in the crowd cheered.

Either the reporter decided to walk away, or the cameraman's shaking hands were directing her.

"This is the most active the crowds have been in a while. I can only speculate that the more bodies are found, the more outlandish the crowd's reaction to the mention of missing sex offenders will be."

"Shelia, do the police believe that the activities within these growing crowds could cause splinter groups to form and openly attack those on the Offender Registry?"

"Lance, that is a good question. I will be speaking to detectives on the case in the next hour." She looked back toward the woods as the camera zoomed in on the movements of the coroner's van. "We will stand by to report more over the next hour."

"Do you think that the police are holding back too much information if they would like assistance from the public?"

"I really cannot answer that." Sheila could not say a word on it, so she answered, "This is the twelfth body that has been found in this same area. We have been out here for two hours, and all I can tell you is that the smell is horrific."

"Yeah, it should be!" I sat up on my knees on the bed and shouted at the television, "I left six pigs out there with the body. How else was that one gonna be found?"

I sat up as soon as I got a good look at the location of my two latest drop sites. This was not my drop site. Someone had interfered in my work. I felt my hands sweating and the hairs on the back of my neck stiffening. The news went on. I smiled and thought about all the steps I had taken when I dropped Mrs. Davenport off last week. I wonder why it took so long for her to be found. Then the thought crossed my mind that someone is disturbing my drop sites. I did think foot traffic by that old house would have led to the body being reported sooner. But then again, who wants their smoking house to be found by the cops? They'll eventually be dragged into the fray. That house was full of cigarette butts and other drug supplies.

"The strangest question that keeps coming up is that there are no witnesses to any vehicle or suspicious persons coming out in these areas. The police say that there are no tire tracks or fingerprints to be found at these sites. We have questioned the FBI, and they are not willing to give us any more information than the police, except to say that this is an ongoing investigation . . . "

"That's amazing," came Lance's brilliant comeback from the station.

" . . . What we could gather from the detectives is that it is likely the same group of serial vigilantes acting in concert. No specific details have been released on this latest body, except that the victim was female. Police are asking us to remind the public that if anyone knows anything, they have several officers dedicated to answering a special tip hotline. They are interested in following any possible leads due to the level of violence involved in these horrid acts."

"'Horrid acts'?" I threw my pillow at the TV. "You ain't seen nothing yet. Wait until six o'clock tonight, baby!" I felt so strong. "You'll get a good scoop."

I left the room. I left the TV on, talking to the walls.

I showered, dressed, and made my way to the library. I have to show my face and get at least two hours of research done on the two papers due at the end of the semester. It's gonna be difficult for them to figure me out. I haven't left an opening for even a single clue to be traced back to me or any of my friends. And even if they get to my circle of friends, they'd hit more dead ends than they could count.

"Hey, Penelope." Mrs. Tucker always has my research requests pulled and waiting for me. The thirty dollars I give her a week doesn't make it hard for her either, which is why she always has my books set aside each week "You at it again, huh?" She smiled at me, and I returned the gesture. "I truly hope you make it as the Valedictorian. You deserve it."

"Thank you, Mrs. Tucker." She was still smiling. "Not that I wouldn't take it. It would be a good token to have, but ten years from now, it would be just another item on my resume." Her smile left. "I'm not being mean. I'm just focused on the future and what I want to accomplish. I want to be one of the best CEO's of one of these Fortune 500 companies."

"Girl, you are more than I thought you were." She pointed at the little reserved table. "I will always have your spot ready for you," she reminded me as she walked away, "I promise you that."

Say it with me . . . *alibi!*

I sat down and got to work. Now that my timeframe for the day was set, I would drop the hint that I was going running and then off to the Daisy Retreat for a session. Thank God for speed-reading and good note-taking skills.

"Hey, Penelope." I think Dr. Warren may have something of a crush on me. "I see you've corrected your last paper. I wish more students would turn in their work early."

"Yes, sir." I smiled at him. He smiled and tried to read my notes. I covered them. "I am trying my best to leave here with a good report."

"That's a good goal. Too bad it's not contagious." He glanced up after I covered my notes. "If only more of my students would take your mindset and ready themselves for the future."

"Thank you." He placed the next assignment on my books. This surprised me. "Thanks for letting me get my grade up to where I need it."

"It's not a problem. You are working on reaching a goal that only two women have achieved in the last thirty years—I would be so proud if you were our next female valedictorian." He smiled again. Way too many smiles—they were starting to aggravate me. "Hey, we are having several students over on Friday night for dinner. Come join us?"

"You said '*we*'?"

"Yes, my partner and I." He looked around before whispering, "You know there are a great deal of people who frown on people like us, much less men like us living together."

"People like us?" The dude was gay. "What time Friday?" He must have thought I was a lesbian. I would laugh, but I was bordering on being mad. It felt good though.

Shoot, I would have to let it pass. I was planning on kicking his ass for smiling at me that much anyway. But this too would work into my plans. I could use his party to complete my purpose in this life.

"Yeah, I'll be there with bells on." I smiled and shuffled my papers so I could get back to work. "I haven't been out in months." I shook my head as I went on, "And a home-cooked meal." He smiled . . . again. "We'll be there," I answered, letting him go on thinking I had a girlfriend.

My phone started to vibrate. This was a good thing.

"Hello?" I answered in the sweetest voice I could. I didn't look back him.

"Penelope, this is Carron." Dr. Warren walked off.

"Yes ma'am." I knew he was leaving slowly so he could hear the start of my conversation. People are generally nosey.

"Penelope, Stanley Franklin was released from prison last week."

"Girl, no!" I tried to sound surprised.

"He is missing. We are doing everything we can to locate him."

"How did he get out three years early?"

"Somehow his prison records got him on the list for release for good behavior. We are trying to locate whoever changed his file."

"Well, what am I going to have to do? I know he doesn't know where I am."

"We don't know that for sure. We have to assume the worst."

"He doesn't have the money to travel two hundred miles to find me on a campus of twenty-three thousand students."

"All he has to do is get on the Internet. Your face and name have constantly been popping up for all the community work you've done and the scholarships you've won."

"What can the Retreat do?"

"They are looking for him." Like I didn't know they were. "We will find him before he gets close to you." The women of the Retreat were all well-connected and very detailed.

"Okay. I am at the library now." I took a breath to give the impression that I was worried about the situation. "I was just heading to the Retreat for kickboxing class anyway."

"Listen, live your life like normal, but stay in touch with your contacts from the Retreat."

"I am and I will."

"I had heard that you were doing better in all your classes there," she paused for a second before adding, "but be careful and watch your back, okay?"

"With all the things I've learned about protecting myself, Stanley will have a face full of pepper spray."

"Okay. I'll talk to you later."

"Bye."

I hung up and gathered my things. I turned on the video link to watch Stanley squirming. I checked to make sure he had water and the Depends on. He'd be ripe by Friday, but time brings about a great deal of good things. I got all excited about seeing him again.

"Ooooh Stanley, I am going to break you off something proper."

"Penelope!" Oh, snap, she heard me.

"Hey Dean Baker, how are you?"

"I didn't know you were . . . active like that." Nosey witch. We would definitely have to have a serious discussion at some point.

"See, you are just listening way too hard." I smiled at her. "Have a great day."

I grabbed my things and walked out of the library. I left no explanation. I should have flattened three of her tires. Hell, I'll stick a pin in that idea. I didn't turn back to see the expression on her face. I took out the folded fifty I had in my pocket and shook Mrs. Tucker's hand, leaving her the money. Her meager paycheck and her husband's social security didn't add up to much, and the money I had taken from those guys needed to find a good home anyway. Her smiles are always enough to remind me that I do have a human side.

———

We arrived at Dr. Warren's. I took Fawn with me and explained to her that they think I am gay. So she laughed until she caught on that she was my date for the night. I do laugh occasionally. The house was an old brick row house. Very quaint. I was still undeterred from the agenda I had planned for the night. We went through all the usual introductions. I insisted on pouring drinks. They were all down ten minutes after dinner was consumed, just after sitting down in the living room to watch *Rent*. I gave them enough to keep them out for at least twelve hours.

———

The drive out to Stanley was a quiet two hours. My dad's old Geo Metro rode pretty good, considering that I had left it parked for two months. I had seen fourteen cars, nine trucks, and three motorcycles. All they would be able to say was that they saw an older woman with a head full of rollers.

I parked a few hundred yards away from the tree house. I left the car parked and started heading east. I walked about two miles before circling back on a slow jog. I startled several of the deer feeders so their hooves would mask my tracks back toward the tree house. I got to the tree house and waited for the movie running in the background, *Cooley High*, to end. I am not that mean. I wanted him to have some type of entertainment to enjoy before our last conversation.

"Hello, Stanley!"

I wish you could have seen the look that covered his face.

"What are you trying to prove having me tied up in this old house?" He sounded a little defiant to me. Must have been that prison mentality. That could be repaired.

"Trying to prove?" I pulled off the wig and dropped the shift I was wearing by the door.

"Trying to prove?" I said again, smiling at him as I placed the glasses on the costume pile. "There is nothing to prove on this night. Just gotta cash the check you wrote four years ago."

"Girl, just face it, you got what you wanted and I got what I wanted." He tried to act as if he were in control. "You should have acted like a woman and broke me off like you were supposed to. That waiting for marriage thing is for the birds and children."

"Oh, I truly plan on acting childish with you tonight." He grunted and tried the leather straps. "Don't worry, you can't break those straps." I pulled the sheet off the table I had set up in the corner. I watched his eyes as he scanned the table of toys. "You have to pay for taking my dad's life."

"Is this all you want me for?" He tried the straps again. "I served my time. They let me out for good behavior."

"No, it wasn't a 'they' thing. I let you out." I moved the water and the jar that had fed him baby food for the past few days. "I hope you have your strength. The bank has a lot of old money it has to give to you." He looked like an overgrown gerbil when he drank from the nozzle of the large bottles.

"Listen here ho, you can't hurt me. The cops will be looking for me." He tried the straps again.

"Are you scared?"

"Ho, I ain't scared of you!" he shouted at me.

I shuddered a little. It made my nerves tighten to remember singing the song my dad requested at his home-going service.

"I'm a ho now?" I put on a pair of latex gloves. "I'm a ho?" I put on a second pair of latex gloves. "Well, this ho has a check for you to sign."

I turned and smiled at him. He tried the straps again. He was scared. *Punk bastard*, I thought as I positioned several pieces of our old Monopoly board on his chest and forehead with Superglue. I pushed a large sponge soaked in honey and vinegar in his mouth. I figured if he was gonna scream, he should choke while he was doing it.

"Stanley, I thought on this mess long and hard. I decided to pay you back in a way that would be fun for you." He grunted as he choked on the sponge's juices. "No, don't speak . . . Just relax and enjoy it." I picked up the bat I had weighted with a toy Hulk Hand attached to the business end in preparation for tonight. "Remember how you told me that before you raped me?" I felt the sweat roll down my neck. "Remember how you loved to come to our house and play board games with my family? Well, they all send their regards." I pulled the mask down over my face. "Tell me which one hurts worse." I swung with my right first.

Cloonk!

The sound the two-pound, cement-filled Hulk Hand bat made was delightful. I connected with the car game piece glued to the right side of his chest. The sound of crushing ribs made me squeal. His coughing, screaming, and strangled hollering at me didn't make much sense.

"What the hell is '*MOUYOOUUN PAC FUH*'?" I asked again, "Can you tell me which hurts the worst, the left-handed swing or the right-handed swing?"

Cloonk!

He screamed and choked.

"Wake the hell up!" I wasn't letting his ass off that easy. "Wake up, punk!" He didn't open his eyes all the way. So I hit him again.

Cloonk! Cloonk! Cloonk!

"Just relax and enjoy it!"

Cloonk! Cloonk! Cloonk!

I think I may have lost my mind for a few minutes.

Cloonk! Cloonk! Cloonk!

"*I got a good-looking daddy!*" I sang the song again.

Cloonk! Cloonk! Cloonk!

"*I got a good-looking daddy!*"

Cloonk! Cloonk! Cloonk!

"Wake up!" I could admit that I had overdone it for a minute. "Dang boy, I forgot you couldn't swang it for long! Sorry, ho!" The boy's eyes rolled back in unconsciousness for a minute. Well, at least until I poured the two-gallon mixture of rubbing alcohol and bleach on his ass. "Where did those Monopoly pieces go to?" They had served their purpose. They were buried in his skin. The only one that remained was the shoe, which sat on his forehead.

He coughed and moaned.

"Just relax and enjoy this, ho."

Cloonk! Cloonk! Cloonk! Cloonk! Cloonk! Cloonk!

"Whew!" I stretched my shoulders with the bat. I felt like I was Barry Bonds and had just hit one out of the park. "Stanley?" I nudged him with the bat. He moved a little. One of the straps had broken during my rampant swinging. He moved to try the straps again in his anguish. So I hit his ass again.

Cloonk! Cloonk

That buried the shoe in his head and stopped all his moving. I stood and waited for a few moments for his chest to rise. When it didn't, I hit his ass a few more times for good measure.

I took his broke-ass to the other side of the lake. That took an hour. I caught myself kicking his body more than dragging it. The oversized boot marks on him and on the plastic would definitely leave the impression that it was several men that had beaten him like this.

———

"Penelope!"

I heard them outside the tree house. I just didn't answer. I just stayed lying there in the corner of the empty room, holding onto my dad's picture.

"Penelope!" I could tell that it was Fawn, Doobie, Lyrix, and Carron. "Penelope!"

I let the noise overtake me. I had taken a Hydrocodone and allowed myself to pass out in the place my dad had built. I heard them talking, but I didn't feel them pick me up.

"Girl, wake up." Carron's breath wasn't all that fresh. Peppermints and coffee do not mix well.

"I am up." I sat up and looked around to see the tree house and my dad's picture. "What in the world?" I was sitting in the workout room of the Daisy Retreat.

"We got you before the police arrived. We knew you would go there since that was your dad's place."

"The police for what?" I said it like I didn't already know.

"How long were you in the tree house?"

"I went there after I took Fawn home from Dr. Warren's. I didn't think Stanley would find me there."

"We checked with Fawn since you guys are tight. She didn't know what to think of any of this. They found Stanley's body four miles from the tree house."

I almost slipped—four miles? That got me thinking, making me woozy all over again.

"What?" I really was thrown. "How? What happened to him?"

"The police think it was the work of the same group of people responsible for the disappearances and murders of the pedophiles in the area. He was beaten something awful and left for dead. "

Doobie cannot hold water.

"I was thinking that you lost your mind and flipped out and beat the hell out of the boy."

"Girl, shut up." She got that in stereo.

"I'm just saying," she said, looking intently at me, "You being all quiet and all. You know how those brainy people tend to flip and kill anyone that has made them upset and mad." I smiled at her. She was the crazy one who had glued a guy's ass to his car. "Anyway," she went on, "they found him in a pool of mud and bleach. There is no way they will get any evidence from that body." She looked around the room, saying, "Ain't nobody gonna miss his tired ass."

I agreed.

"Where is my mother?" I looked at Lyrix and Carron. "Have you guys called her?"

"She's on her way here now." She clutched my hand. "We haven't heard from your sisters, but your brother said he would find them and they would be here as soon as they could."

"Okay." I was fine. I didn't feel pushed or rushed. I hadn't felt that way in a long time. "Where is everyone at today? Shouldn't there be a class in here right now?"

"You, us, and twenty-six other women are doing a Tae Bo class right now."

"Okay, I got you."

The door opened and the group walked in. They hugged me, and I let them think that they were comforting me. I played the role I had been playing for a long time. We sat around, listened to music, talked, laughed, and relaxed for a change. All of these women would have done the same thing I had done to Stanley, but I don't believe most of them could keep it inside for very long. Mother showed up and hugged me like she hadn't just seen me at the Labor Day picnic. Three months doesn't make you miss someone that much. She joined into the conversations and seemed to know a great many of the women in the room. All I could think was *wow*. My mom must have been connected to the Retreat herself.

When my sisters walked, in I noticed the dirt on their tennis shoes. Then I realized who must have moved Stanley's dead-pan ass. They both hugged me.

"I know what you guys have done," I whispered into their ears, "Don't say a word to me about nothing." They pulled back and looked me in the face as I explained, "I see the dirt on your shoes." I pretended to cry. "Thank you for having my back." Then it turned into a real cry of relief. I was never alone.

The room filled with women crying on each other. I saw my brother walk in. He nodded at me and then walked out as quickly as he had come in. Life is good when you realize family has always had your back. I smiled as I thought about the words I had learned alongside my sisters: *"We will not stand broken and defeated. We will plant our roots deeper. Our petals shall be stronger than they were before. We shall overcome by planting daisies and sowing new seeds to reap the bountiful harvest."*

This book is dedicated to all the staff of:

Bay Area Turning Point
Women's Rescue Center
Webster, Texas
http://www.bayareaturningpoint.org

Please make a donation of $10.00 here or to your nearest
women's rescue center.

Lightning Source UK Ltd.
Milton Keynes UK
UKOW05f0302091014

239768UK00002B/122/P